MINE TO Share

MINE (TO *Share*

A NOVEL

DEBBIE GILLILAND

AMBASSADOR INTERNATIONAL
GREENVILLE, SOUTH CAROLINA & BELFAST, NORTHERN IRELAND

www.ambassador-international.com

Mine to Share

ISBN: 978-1-64960-434-7
eISBN: 978-1-64960-482-8

Cover design by Hannah Linder Designs
Interior typesetting by Dentelle Design
Edited by Ashley Dill

AMBASSADOR INTERNATIONAL
Emerald House Group, Inc.
411 University Ridge, Suite B14
Greenville, SC 29601
United States
www.ambassador-international.com

AMBASSADOR BOOKS
The Mount
2 Woodstock Link
Belfast, BT6 8DD
Northern Ireland, United Kingdom
www.ambassadormedia.co.uk

The colophon is a trademark of Ambassador, a Christian publishing company.

Thank you to my readers,
who have encouraged me to continue the stories
of the characters in this book.
May you experience both their joys and their sorrows
and know that the love and forgiveness God grants to them
is available to all of us in equal measure.

CHAPTER ONE

THE EARLY MORNING SUNSHINE PEEKED through the mini blinds and tiptoed in stripes across Jannah's bedroom floor. Tucker was asleep on the rug beside the child's bed. The yellow lab had slept there since joining the family three years earlier. Jannah was five years old then, and the two became inseparable companions. Tucker was no longer the rambunctious puppy who greeted every visitor with a slobbery welcome, and his loyalty to Miss Jannah grew fiercer with every passing year.

Noise from the kitchen awakened Tucker. He stretched on the floor and then stood to shake off his morning laziness. He was tall enough now to lay his head near Jannah's pillow without jumping onto the bed. However, he had no patience this morning and began to nuzzle the girl. Jannah protested by pulling the covers over her head, but Tucker tugged them away from her face.

"Tucker! It's Saturday." Jannah moaned. Tucker cocked his head and looked at her with dark brown eyes, begging to play. Admitting defeat, Jannah threw off the covers and sat on the end of her bed.

Tucker jumped and rested his front legs around Jannah's. She wrapped her arms around his neck and hugged him close. A wide yawn caverned across her face, and she stretched her arms high over her head.

"Next Saturday, I will make you sleep outside my bedroom door, and then I can sleep as late as I want!" Then, she giggled. She knew she would never forbid Tucker to sleep at her bedside. Indeed, she would toss and turn without him there!

"Looks like it is going to be a sunny day," Jannah said as she pulled summer clothes from her closet. She shimmied out of her pajamas and stuffed her long arms and legs into the shorts and shirt. She grabbed a brush from her dresser and began coaxing snags from her shoulder-length hair. Little fingers twisted a hair tie around her brown hair, pulling it back from her freckled face in a messy pigtail. Mom would comb through it after breakfast, and the hair tie would then hold the hair in a smooth and snug grip.

Tucker sat and watched the girl impatiently, his long tongue hanging out in anticipation of the day ahead.

JANNAH PUSHED THROUGH THE FRONT door and greeted the warm morning with an enthusiastic grin. "Let's go, Tucker!" she said as the dog rushed past her and into the green grass. His nose immediately dipped to catch the trail of a rabbit skittering off into the bushes at the back of their property. He took off in hot pursuit, and Jannah called after him. When she realized nothing she could say would discourage him, Jannah sat down on the front step waiting for him to return from his hunt.

She looked across her yard to Grandpa Hawkeye's property. Her grandpa, James Hawthorne, moved into the house next door two years ago. Jannah remembered the first time she had spoken to him when he walked past her house. That was before she found out he was her grandpa. She had misunderstood his last name, and the resulting misnomer for the older man stuck. To Jannah, he was "Grandpa Hawkeye."

The flowerbeds in the next yard were coming alive with splashes of color in the greenery. Clematis vines were already inching up the trellises framing the largest flowerbed. It was one of her favorite times of the year because she would spend hours helping Grandpa pull weeds and deadhead the blooms.

She giggled to herself, remembering Grandpa telling her how she did not know the difference between a flower and a weed the first summer she helped him. That was two years ago, though; and now, she could identify lilies, iris, lilacs, crocus, clematis, and many other flowers there were to tend.

Where was Grandpa Hawkeye this morning, anyway? He usually watered his flowers early in the mornings when it was cooler. And where was Tucker? Thinking about the flowerbeds had distracted her, and now the dog was nowhere to be seen!

"Tucker!" she shouted. Jannah stood and jogged to the backyard, calling his name a second time. Still no response—and no sight of him either. A knot formed in her stomach. Tucker had never wandered out of their yard so far he did not come running when she called to him.

"Tucker, where are you?" This time, fear muted her voice. Her eyes swept along the brushy border where he had disappeared, but not a leaf moved. Jannah stood frozen in place, straining to hear any response from the missing dog.

Wait! She did hear something! Was that a distressed whimper she heard coming from down the road? Jannah bolted to the front yard and down the sidewalk toward the busy street. She halted to listen for the cry again.

"Tucker?" she shouted. "Where are you?" Her heart pulled her both east and west for fear of choosing the wrong direction.

Then she saw him. Tucker was lying at the side of the road in so much pain, he could not lift his head. A man knelt beside the dog, whispering to calm the injured animal. Her heart pounded wildly in her chest.

"Tucker!" she shouted again as her legs raced down the sidewalk.

The man turned toward her but did not move from the dog's side. He motioned for Jannah to come closer. "He ran out into the street and was grazed by a truck. I don't think the truck driver even realized it. We shouldn't move the dog without a sling. He might have internal injuries we can't see."

Jannah collapsed to her knees on the ground next to him. She lifted her head to look into the face of the stranger who had taken command. Her eyes begged permission to touch her own dog.

The man nodded, then added, "Just be careful. We don't want to cause him more pain."

Jannah bent over to touch her cheek to Tucker's head. "Oh, Tucker!" she whispered. "I love you so much!" Her slim fingers stroked the dog's neck.

She sat up again and dared to look at the limp body. Her eyes widened in horror when she saw Tucker's left hind leg bleeding and bent at an unnatural angle.

The man watched her. "Do you live far from here?" he asked.

"No," Jannah responded in a whisper. "We live just a couple blocks away."

"Could you run to your house and find a bed sheet?"

"What would you do with a sheet?" Jannah asked.

"We would put your dog on the sheet to carry him," the man explained. "Is there anyone at your house who could help us lift the dog?"

"Oh! Yes! I can go get Grandpa Hawkeye!" Jannah jumped up, anxious to do something to help Tucker. "Can you stay here with Tucker until I get back?"

The man smiled at her question. "I won't go anywhere," he assured her.

Jannah ran faster than she ever had. She tore open the front door and shouted for her mother. "I need a bed sheet, Mommy! Tucker got hit by a truck!"

"What?" her mother responded from the laundry room. "What happened?" She hurried to the kitchen with unfolded clothes heaped in her arms. She dropped the laundry onto the table and cocked her head toward Jannah as the story tumbled out of quivering lips.

"Tucker ran off when we went outside this morning, and I guess I let him get too far away." Jannah's eyes filled with tears again at the thought of the part she had played in the accident. If only she had kept her eyes on Tucker and not let him wander off. "I need to go get Grandpa. The man said he needs someone who can help us lift Tucker."

Jannah was out the door before her mother could question her further. It only took a few minutes for Jannah to find Grandpa Hawkeye on his knees in a flowerbed at the rear of his property. He struggled to his feet and swatted the loose dirt from his pants. Jannah grabbed his hand and pulled him across the lawn while she explained the urgency between sobs. Marta had found an old sheet they used for camping and was backing the car out of the garage.

"Tucker is only a couple blocks away, Mommy," Jannah said as she jumped into the back seat. "Why are we taking the van?"

"We will probably need the van to get to the veterinarian," her mom explained. "Which direction do I go at the stop sign?"

"Go right," Jannah directed, her voice shaking with emotion. In the presence of the two adults who guarded her life, Jannah broke into tears. "I'm so sorry, Mommy! I should not have let Tucker out of our yard!"

Grandpa climbed into the back seat opposite Jannah. He reached across the seat and gathered her tiny hand in his.

"Jannah, no one could keep Tucker in sight all the time. He loves to run and chase smells. Let's concentrate on getting him the care he needs right now, okay?" Her mother's words were barely comforting.

Grandpa squeezed Jannah's hand as they pulled up to the curb where Tucker was lying.

As the stranger had promised, he had not left the dog's side. He looked up when the van stopped. Mom gathered up the bed sheet and hurried to catch up with Grandpa and Jannah. Tucker was muzzled with a rolled handkerchief.

"Even the gentlest dogs can try to bite if they are in pain," the man explained. "The handkerchief will not hurt him, and it will keep all of us safe."

"My daughter told us to bring a bed sheet. How can we help?"

The man motioned for Mom to spread the sheet on the grass beside the curb. Glancing at Grandpa, he instructed, "At the count of three, you lift his head and shoulders. I will lift his hips and hind legs, and we will place him on the sheet. He will probably struggle because there will be pain, but we need to get him x-rayed soon to know what his injuries are." Grandpa nodded his head and knelt in place.

"One. Two. Three. Lift!" The two men gently lifted the wounded dog and placed him on the sheet. An anguished moan escaped Tucker's muzzled mouth, but he did not struggle.

"Now, we need to get him into your van," one of the men instructed. Motioning to her mom, he directed her to back the van closer to where Tucker lay on the grass. Traffic slowed as vehicles moved past the scene.

"We will do a three-count again," the stranger said to James when the van was in place. "It will be a higher lift to get him into the van. Ready?"

"Ready!" Grandpa responded.

Again, Tucker whimpered in pain while being moved, but he soon settled down on the blood-stained sheet. His big, brown eyes looked mournfully at Jannah.

"Thank you so much for your help," Mom said to the man. "I don't know what Jannah would have done if you had not been here to help her!"

"No problem. My name is Pat Watson." The man lifted his ball cap and smoothed back his dark hair, then settled the cap back into place. He dusted the seat of his shorts and stomped the dirt from the curb off his shoes. "I was just doing my morning jog when I saw him run out into the road. As I told your daughter, I don't think the truck driver even knew he had hit a dog. At least, I'd like to think he would have stopped had he known."

"Thank you, Pat. I guess we need to get Tucker to our vet. His office is quite a ways from here."

The man smiled and said, "Well, I happen to be a vet, and my clinic is just a few blocks away. I would be glad to get some x-rays and help determine the injuries."

"You're a vet?" her mom asked. "No wonder you knew exactly how to handle an injured dog! We are even more fortunate than I thought to have you help us! I am fine with taking Tucker to your clinic. Do you want to ride with us?"

"Sure!' the doctor replied. He hopped into the passenger's seat and directed them to his clinic.

Dr. Watson jumped out and hurried inside when Mom pulled up next to the building. An assistant returned with him, carrying a stretcher board. Together, they transferred Tucker with the sheet onto the board, whispering to the animal to keep him calm.

"Follow us inside," Dr. Watson said, watching as they loaded Tucker onto the board. "You can have a seat in the waiting room while we get some x-rays, and then I will be right out with the results."

Mom and Grandpa sat at opposite ends of a couch with Jannah perched between them. Jannah could not relax. She fiddled with her hands and never moved her gaze from the exam room door.

"What is taking so long?" Jannah whispered.

Marta tried to smile. "It hasn't been that long," she replied. She put an arm around the girl's slender shoulders and pulled her close. "Scoot back and let me cuddle with you."

Jannah pushed herself back onto the couch and leaned into her mother's side. Marta buried her nose in Jannah's soft hair. She saw the concern in the vet's eyes as he handled Tucker. *How will Jannah react if the vet's advice is to put the animal down?* Jannah had survived worse scenarios, but this might be the tragedy that finally broke her childhood spirit.

Marta glanced at James and found him watching Jannah, no doubt feeling as helpless as she felt, knowing this was yet another sorrow for someone so young to shoulder. Perhaps James was praying this very minute for his God to spare Tucker's life. That would be like him—always praying for some kind of Divine intervention in the lives of those he loved. Marta was certain James had been praying for her and Jannah long before he admitted he was her biological father.

Finally, the hallway door opened, and Dr. Watson stepped back into the waiting room wearing a white doctor's jacket over his jogging outfit. He walked over to Jannah and knelt in front of her before saying a word. He took her hand in his and patted it gently.

"Tucker is pretty badly injured in his left hindquarter. I looked at the x-rays very closely so I could give you all the options possible, but I think the injury is too extensive to heal correctly." He paused, and Marta braced herself for the worst. "If Tucker were my dog, I would amputate the injured leg and help him learn to get around on three legs. He would never walk or run normally again with a crippled fourth leg, but most dogs adapt well to life with three legs."

Jannah listened quietly. She shook her head, denying all that had happened in the last couple of hours. Marta pulled her daughter close again and breathed a deep sigh. Another heartbreak for this child!

James finally broke the silence with a question Marta wanted to ask. "Are you certain you cannot save Tucker's leg?"

Dr. Watson stood and pulled an empty chair closer to the family. "Well, I did look over the x-rays very closely. The leg could be pinned in three different places, but recovery from such a surgery would require several weeks of immobilization; and Tucker doesn't strike me as the kind of dog who enjoys sitting around." He smiled gently at Jannah.

"What kind of recovery time would you expect with an amputation?" James asked.

"Most dogs are up and walking within a day of surgery," Dr. Watson responded. "They can be given pain medicine, just like humans, but we don't want to continue that any longer than necessary. The biggest challenge a dog faces when it loses a limb," Dr. Watson continued, "is to relearn proprioception, which means it needs to get a new idea of where its body is in space and how to balance—like the bubble in a level. The most important challenge for the dog's owner is to protect the remaining limbs. Often, people will let the dog overdo it and end up putting undue stress on the dog's joints, leading to further injuries and arthritis."

James turned and looked at Marta. After a moment, Dr. Watson said, "You are welcome to take the x-rays to your family vet and see what his advice would be. I understand you have only just met me, and I would want you to be in complete agreement before we make any decisions. I don't know your family vet, but I would guess he would prefer to see the x-rays and would not advise you to move Tucker until a decision is made." He paused before adding, "He could certainly call me and discuss the options I have offered you."

Marta sighed heavily and looked at the floor. How much would this kind of surgery cost? She was having trouble enough covering the essential expenses of daily life. The bank had been lenient with her late house payments for several months after her husband's suicide while she was dealing with settling his financial matters. Still, how could she deny Tucker a chance for recovery from this accident? Indeed, how could she ever explain to Jannah they could not afford the proper care for her dearest friend? She could not!

"I think we need to let you get back to helping Tucker feel better," Marta responded. "I don't think we should move Tucker at this point. I know you will do everything you can to keep his pain controlled." She turned to look at James. "What do you think?"

James reached to hold Jannah's hand. "I agree," he replied, keeping his eyes on the child's face. "Can the amputation surgery be done right away?"

Dr. Watson leaned into the small group and smiled. "I will have Laurie reschedule my morning appointments, and we will get started right away."

"Could I see Tucker first?" Jannah whispered.

"Of course," Dr. Watson answered. He stood and held a hand out toward Jannah. "We did give him a shot to keep him calm, so he will seem sleepy. We will peek at him, and then I will have you wait out here."

Jannah walked with the doctor toward the exam room. Marta and James followed close behind. Inside, Tucker was lying on his side on a table beneath a bright light. A vet assistant stood beside him, petting him gently between his ears. Tucker lifted his head when Jannah walked in, and she rushed to Tucker's side.

"Oh, Tucker! I am so sorry I let you out of my sight!" she sobbed. The dog licked her hand as she reached to stroke his face.

Dr. Watson hurried to stand beside Jannah, ready to restrain her if she moved to embrace the dog and cause him to attempt to stand. He bent over to talk to the child. "Tucker will never blame you, Jannah. He was just doing what a dog loves to do—running!" Tears bobbed at the brims of Jannah's eyes. "Let's get you back out to the waiting room, and I will get him all fixed up for you. He will be able to run and play with you again; wait and see!"

"Let's go, Jannah," James said quietly. The girl took his hand and walked away from Tucker. Marta followed them to the waiting room. James was there to comfort her daughter time and again. Marta imagined she could hear the quick prayer James must have uttered on their behalf. She envied his calm confidence as he ushered Jannah from the exam room.

SEVERAL PEOPLE CAME AND WENT from the vet's waiting room, carrying or leading pets on leashes. Marta mentally calculated the expense the owners were incurring, all for the love of an animal. She should have asked the vet what the charge would be for the surgery Tucker was having. But then James would have heard the anxiety in her voice and suspected the financial worries Marta had not shared with him.

She would have to ask her parents for help if the cost was too great. Unfortunately, she had not talked to them about her situation either. Why did this have to happen now?

She glanced at Jannah, cuddled up with James on the couch opposite her. Jannah was too old to sit on anyone's lap, but she planted herself as close to James as possible. Marta smiled when she saw the child's hand tucked into James'.

"How long has it been, Mommy?" Jannah asked in a whisper.

Marta checked her watch. "An hour and a half," she answered.

"It seems like *forever!*" Jannah responded. "Do you think they are almost done?"

The exam room door opened as if on cue, and Dr. Watson hurried toward them. "All done!" he announced. "The surgery went very well. Tucker is still asleep, but he will be just fine."

Jannah bounced up off the couch. "Can I see him now?"

"Not right now," Dr. Watson cautioned. "We will keep a close eye on him until the sedative wears off. Why don't you all come back later this afternoon? Tucker should be able to see you then."

Jannah's shoulders drooped. "Hey, Jannah, you can help me with some things in the flower garden for a while." James nudged her shoulder. "Then we will come back here and check on Tucker."

"Yes," Marta added. "We need to go find some lunch. I heard your stomach growling a few minutes ago, Jannah!"

Dr. Watson knelt in front of the girl. "Tucker is going to be fine! I promise to take good care of him. You go eat lunch and then come back in a few hours, okay?" He stood and moved to talk to Marta. "We will keep Tucker here overnight if that works for you. Then we will coax him up in the morning and work with him to figure out his balance. At the end of the day tomorrow, you can come to get him, and we will show you how to care for his incision and how to watch for infection. We will also show you how to help him exercise and keep moving to prevent stiffness."

"Thank you so much for all you have done." Marta lifted her hand, offering a handshake. "You certainly were in the right place when we needed you this morning!"

Dr. Watson wrapped Marta's hand in his. "I am glad I could help. I am confident we made the right decision about the surgery. Tucker will be up and running in no time at all."

CHAPTER TWO

DONNA HEAVED A DEEP SIGH as she settled down into her recliner. Her evening walk around her neighborhood had left her exhausted. Still, her progress made her proud. Two years ago, she had neither the motivation nor the ability to step outside her home. She smiled as she glanced around the room. She had dusted and vacuumed earlier in the day, and the tidy room beckoned her to sit and rest.

The divorce had taken its toll on her—physically and emotionally. Her identity in life had been "Dr. Wright's wife" for twenty years. But the title had been stripped from her and handed over to a petite and much younger woman. The man she had married and supported through medical school was free to begin a new life with a woman who was young enough to be his daughter.

Donna's self-esteem had withered and died as she gained weight. Complications from back surgery had left her stooped. She had felt like a prisoner in her home, dependent upon a walker to move around in the house awarded to her as part of the settlement.

Donna shuddered as she recalled the desolation that had controlled her. Breathing itself had become a chore, one she would have readily relinquished. Her heart had grown bitter. Even her children had begun to offer lame excuses for keeping their distance.

But then one day, James Hawthorne had visited. James was the father of the baby girl Donna had placed for adoption during her senior year of high school—the year that marked the most regretted decision of her life. April 14 was the child's birthday, but not a single day in the last forty-six years had passed without thinking of that daughter.

In her bitterness, Donna had tried to shut the door against him until he had quietly told her he had brought pictures of her daughter and granddaughter. Donna opened the door to allow James into her home, as her maternal instincts had taken over. A simple signature on the adoption forms all those years ago could not quell the questions that had swirled in her heart for so many years.

Had her adoptive parents loved her—really loved her? Where had she lived? Had she done well in school? Did she know she had been placed for adoption? Had she married? Had she had children of her own? Had she chosen a career? Had she looked for her biological parents?

Donna reached over to the end table by her chair and picked up the double frame holding the two pictures James had given her that day—Marta and Jannah. They were *her* family. The need to touch their lives drew her finger over the glass that covered the images.

Their conversation that day had taken an unexpected turn when James began talking about his God. James had dared suggest God cared about her. And then he had gone to his car to get his Bible. He had shown her the plan God offered to make Donna part of His family. She had found the Bible on her coffee table hours after James left for home.

Intrigued by James' unabashed certainty of God's love, she had picked up the Bible daily to read through a chapter or two. Much of it she had not understood, but she read verse after verse and was convinced there was a God Who had created her and loved *her*!

This truth had provided a reason to live again. It had motivated her to get up in the morning, get dressed, and eat properly. Donna had made an appointment with her doctor and begun a grueling round of physical therapy, strengthening her legs. After months of treatment and faithfully completing her home exercises, Donna had folded up her walker and put it in the back of the closet. Now, she looked forward to her daily walk around four neighborhood blocks. It wasn't much, but it was so much more than she had been able to do before!

The end of the day left Donna tired. She returned the photo frame to the table and stood to go to her bedroom. James had said she might someday get to meet her daughter and granddaughter. Perhaps she would!

CHAPTER THREE

JANNAH NIBBLED ON THE SANDWICH Mom fixed when they got home from the clinic. It was like cotton in her mouth, and her stomach twisted. She remembered feeling the exact same way after her father died. It had taken a very long time for her to look forward to a meal. Today, Jannah ate because she knew her mother would insist she eat, and she could not bear the thought of causing her mother more distress.

Had she imagined it, or was there a shadow of sadness following her mom around lately? She smiled often enough, but it was never one of the glowing smiles Jannah remembered from the past. How long had it been since Mommy had laughed as if someone had tickled her? *Really* laughed? Did she still miss Jake and their daddy as much as Jannah did?

Mom sat on the stool opposite Jannah and took a bite of the sandwich she had fixed for herself. The bar off the kitchen was a sunny spot where the two ate most of their meals together.

"Tucker is going to be fine, honey," she said, jolting the child's thoughts back to the dining room.

Jannah swallowed the bite lodged in her throat. "I hope so," she whispered. "It seems so odd without him here."

"I am sure Tucker is missing you, too." Mom took a sip of her tea. "Why don't you see what kind of help Grandpa Hawkeye needs, and then we will go back to check on Tucker in a few hours?"

Jannah pushed away from the table and helped carry the dishes to the sink. She grabbed her gardening gloves at the back door and headed to Grandpa's house across the lawn. The door slammed at her heels. She decided to use this opportunity to talk to him about her mother.

"Hi, Grandpa!" Jannah waved as she neared the man squatting next to one of his garden beds.

"Hey, there!" He offered her a big smile. "Did you have some lunch?"

"Mom fixed me a sandwich, but I couldn't eat it all."

He stood and dusted the soil off his hands. "You are worried about Tucker, aren't you?" He held out an arm, offering Jannah a hug. She wrapped her arms around the old man and buried her face in his shirt while he patted her back. "He's going to be fine, Jannah. I think God put Dr. Watson right where he was this morning so he could be the one to take care of Tucker."

"But why did God let Tucker get hit in the first place?" Jannah asked. She looked up at him, her eyes squinted and her nose wrinkled up in confusion.

Grandpa looked away. "I can't answer that, Jannah," he admitted. "But I do know God will hear our prayers for Tucker. When Tucker comes home and can run and play again, we will understand better how much God loves us."

"Have you prayed for Tucker?"

"Of course, I have!" he answered. "When you came and asked me to help this morning, I prayed all the way to Tucker's side that God would take care of him. I think the fact Dr. Watson was right there was one way God proved He was watching out for Tucker."

"I just don't understand why Tucker ran out of our yard," Jannah whispered. "He never does that!"

He patted the child's shoulders. "Oh, Tucker might have heard or smelled something you and I would not have noticed. And even though he is trained to stay in your yard unless you are with him, his instincts to run and chase took over." Grandpa paused, but Jannah was silent.

"Ready to help me clean the leaves out of this bed?" he asked. "I think we will find some green lily shoots trying to poke up through all the dried leaves." He pulled the bucket close to their work area and squatted down to get started.

Jannah pulled on her gloves and dropped to her knees. She gathered a handful of leaves and dropped them into the bucket, uncovering a clump of green stems. Her fingers combed debris away from the tender plant like Grandpa Hawkeye had shown her two years ago. He worked beside her, moving from plant to plant.

Jannah leaned back and sat on her heels. "Does Mommy seem okay to you?"

"What do you mean?"

"Well, she seems sad to me—all the time." Jannah patted her gloves together to knock off some soil and then leaned forward to resume her work.

Grandpa rocked back to sit on his heels. "Are *you* sad a lot of the time? Sometimes when we are sad ourselves, it seems like everyone around us is sad, too."

Jannah's nose wrinkled in thought. "Maybe *sad* isn't the right word," she offered. "Maybe it is more that she seems worried all the time."

"What do you think she is worried about?" he prodded.

"I don't know. Maybe you could talk to Mommy and see if she will tell you."

"Consider it done!" He leaned back into the flower garden. "Let's work another thirty minutes; then, we can clean up and visit Tucker. I predict he will feel better and be glad to see us!"

JANNAH JUMPED OUT OF THE van and hurried to the vet clinic door. She hopped from foot to foot waiting for Grandpa Hawkeye and her mother to catch up. She tugged at the heavy door until Grandpa took over and opened it.

Dr. Watson was behind the counter visiting with his receptionist. A broad smile danced across his face when he saw the Newtons entering. "I was hoping you would be here soon," he greeted them. "Tucker is awake and doing very well. I think he will be happy to see you all. Come on back, and we will go see him."

Jannah had no trouble pushing through the waiting room door. By that time, the doctor was in the hallway and motioned for them to follow him.

"We have had Tucker up and standing already," he reported. "We have a 'buggy' device we use to help dogs regain their balance after a surgery like this. Tucker figured it out right away!" He opened an exam room door and held it for the family to enter.

Tucker struggled to stand when he saw Jannah. It was awkward for him, but he found his legs and barked a greeting. Jannah froze in the doorway and stared at the dog's bandaged side where the injured leg had been. Behind her, Mom and Grandpa waited for the girl to become comfortable with the sight of her dog.

"Come on in," Dr. Watson encouraged. "Tucker is ready for some hugs!"

Jannah inched closer but hesitated before she was close enough to touch the dog. She sucked in a deep breath and bit her bottom lip. Her brown eyes brimmed with tears. Grandpa stepped up beside her and put his arm around her stiffened shoulders. "Dr. Watson said it is okay to give Tucker a hug. What are we waiting for?" he asked. He took her hand and gently tugged her forward.

Tucker barked a second time, and this time, Jannah ran to him and dropped to her knees. She put her small hands on the dog's face and rubbed his jowls with her thumbs. "Oh, Tucker! I am so glad you are going to be all right!" she sobbed. Tucker licked her fingers and nuzzled into her neck, but there was none of the usual frenzied wagging of his hindquarters when Jannah was near him.

Grandpa knelt beside Jannah and patted Tucker's head. "Hey, Tucker! You gave us all quite a scare!" The dog's tongue lopped over the side of his jaw as he patted him. His dark brown eyes begged for forgiveness, and Grandpa could not withhold it. "We love you, Buddy!"

Dr. Watson observed the reunion from the door. After a few minutes, he stepped closer and touched Mommy's arm to urge her into the group near the dog. "Tucker is going to stay here with us for the night, but he will be ready to go home in the morning. When you come to get him, I will remove his bandage and show you how to clean the wound. The important thing is to keep the wound clean and dry. You will probably want to keep Tucker inside until the stitches are removed in two weeks. Exercise is also very important. Tucker will need to keep moving but not too much. Overexertion will prolong his recovery."

Mom ran her hand through her hair and shook her head. "You will do fine," Dr. Watson assured her with a smile. "Tucker is a very healthy dog, and he is going to heal quickly."

"Thank you again for all you have done for Tucker today," Mother responded.

"Glad I could help," Dr. Watson answered. "Spend whatever time you want here with Tucker now, and I will see you again in the morning."

CHAPTER FOUR

DR. PAT WATSON SAT AT his desk, thumbing through the day's mail. He could hear the Newtons talking to Tucker in the next room. Tucker would be in good hands when he went home tomorrow. His was a happy ending to a near tragedy. Pat shook his head, revisiting the scene of the accident that morning. The experience reminded him of another accident—one which had not ended happily at all.

He closed his eyes and took a deep breath, trying to block the unwanted memory. Pat had tried every coping strategy to erase the images of the child lying on the side of the road. He could still feel the small hand in his own, hear the distant sirens, and sense the child's life slipping away.

Pat was on his way to the clinic that horrible morning. When he saw the boy run into the street chasing a kitten, he pounded a too-late warning honk from the car and slammed on his breaks. The child's mother ran from the house, shouting her son's name over and over and over. Pat jumped out of the car and rushed to the mother's side as she knelt over the limp body.

"Don't move him!" Pat instructed as he approached. "We need to call for an ambulance." He was already dialing nine-one-one on his phone.

Waiting for the ambulance alongside the inconsolable mother were the longest moments of Pat's life. He begged God to spare the little boy, but it was too late. The head injuries had robbed him of life.

The mother clung to the little body, moaning in guttural anguish. Tears streaked Pat's face as he helplessly watched the EMTs lift the woman from the ground and hold her. Her son was gone, and their mission now was to comfort her.

A police officer approached Pat and asked if he had been driving the car that hit the boy. Pat could hardly respond. Numbness had squelched his reasoning, and the questions sounded like a blur against the traffic's din. He managed to nod his head.

"There was a kitten," Pat explained. "He was chasing a tiny kitten, and I didn't see either one of them until it was too late. I am so sorry." More tears fell. "I need to go talk to her, tell her how sorry I am." Pat's chin trembled as he peered through the congestion of emergency vehicles and responders.

"She has corroborated your story, sir," the office reassured quietly. "She told us she saw it all happen, but she couldn't get out the door in time to stop him."

Reliving the memories of that day tortured Pat every time. He dropped his head to his desk and unleashed the sobs that flooded his heart. Why did *he* have to be the one to hit the little boy? The prospect of ever experiencing the grief of that boy's mother was too much for him to imagine. He swore he'd never get close to a child or risk being a parent. Pat's own grief for the boy was too much to carry, and he wasn't even the father. How could he lose one of his own?

CHAPTER FIVE

CARING FOR TUCKER'S WOUND GREW easier for Marta. Initially, seeing the wound at the clinic was startling. There were so many stitches! James offered to come help the first few times the bandage was removed. Jannah cringed at the sight, so her job was to whisper to Tucker and keep him calm.

Jannah also helped with Tucker's exercising. Finding ways for him to move around inside was difficult. She walked the dog in circles around the living room, walked him through the kitchen, and helped him up and down the basement steps. Jannah was patient and a natural encourager. She spoke sweetly to him, rubbing his back when he stumbled. Tucker resisted movement some days, but Jannah would cup his head in her small hands and put her forehead against his. They seemed to have a silent understanding, and she always got Tucker on his feet.

After two weeks of recuperation, Marta and Jannah loaded Tucker into the van to see Dr. Watson and have his stitches removed. Marta was eager for Tucker to heal; she did not like changing bandages! Jannah hoped Dr. Watson would allow Tucker to go outside again. It had been a long two weeks!

On their walk across the parking lot, Jannah felt Tucker sucking in the fresh outside air. She had missed being outside, too. She stayed by Tucker's side as they entered the clinic. Dr. Watson asked them to keep Tucker on a leash so he wouldn't run off in excitement or approach any other animals in the waiting room.

After checking in, Jannah and Marta took seats facing the door Dr. Watson would open. Tucker settled down on the floor at their feet. He was learning how to navigate on three legs, although it was awkward at times. His tortured moaning had finally stopped. Overall, he was doing so much better.

Marta noticed a younger child whispering to his mother and pointing at Tucker. The mother shushed him and pushed his pointing finger into his lap. She smiled nervously, silently apologizing. For the first time, Marta realized others would see Tucker differently now and hoped Jannah wouldn't feel discouraged by the fact. Jannah slipped out of the chair and onto the floor beside her dog. She wrapped her arms around his neck.

"Tucker, we are ready for you." Dr. Watson stepped through the door. He watched as Tucker struggled up and forward. "Come on in, Tucker! It looks like you are getting along very well!"

They all followed Dr. Watson back, and Jannah was relieved to be outside of the busy waiting room!

"Any problems you are aware of?" Dr. Watson asked Marta.

Marta nodded toward Tucker standing at the doctor's feet. "No. We've made it through two weeks of dressing changes, and Jannah has been walking him all around the house. We've done our best to take care of him."

Dr. Watson knelt at Tucker's head, rubbing him behind the ears. Tucker's tongue hung out of his mouth in open appreciation of the doctor's touch. "Let's get him up here on the table, and we will take a look at the incision." An assistant helped Dr. Watson lift Tucker onto the exam table. They removed the dressing and inspected the healing wound.

"I am impressed!" He turned and grinned at Marta. "Would you be interested in a job here at the clinic?"

"No way!" Marta sputtered, raising her hands in front of her. "I couldn't have dealt with all those bandages for anyone except Tucker!"

"You did a fine job!" the vet replied. "I am going to let you two go back to the waiting room while we remove the stitches, and then we will send you home for a couple more weeks of wound care. After that, Tucker should be almost as good as new!"

Jannah twisted her fingers together as she listened. "Can I take him outside to play yet?"

"Let me look at the incision before I answer." Dr. Watson patted Jannah's shoulders. "Do you think he has missed being outside?" He winked at Marta while he waited for Jannah's response.

"Oh, yes!" Jannah's eyes sparkled, and she appeared hopeful. "He really didn't want to get into the van when we came here. He wanted to stay outside and play in the yard."

"I'll let you know what I think in just a few minutes, okay?"

Marta took Jannah's hand and led her to the door.

"Why don't you wait in my office?" Dr. Watson suggested. "It's just across the hall. It will only take a few minutes to get these stitches out."

His office was small. The desk and filing cabinet consumed most of the space. Marta and Jannah settled down into the two chairs facing the desk. On the wall behind the desk, a large photograph of a mare and her new foal framed the words, "Nature displays the goodness of God." A neatly stacked pile of papers framed one side of the desk, and a couple thick books balanced the other side.

"He's a nice guy, isn't he, Mommy?" Jannah whispered.

"Dr. Watson?" Marta asked. Jannah nodded with a tender smile. "He is a very nice man and a good veterinarian. Tucker seems to like him, for sure!"

"Can we bring Tucker here for all his shots?"

Marta bit her lip. "We'll see, dear. He's already done a lot for Tucker!"

Pat scrubbed and dried his hands after the examination. The Newtons would be happy to hear his instructions for limited outside play and much simpler wound care. It was clear the family cared about their dog.

He stepped across the hallway and into his office. "Thanks for waiting here." His voice pulled two anxious faces toward him. "Tucker is all ready to go! You two have done a remarkable job keeping his wound clean! He is moving much easier than most dogs do after a procedure like that. Good job!"

Marta stood, holding her hand out for the doctor. "We appreciate everything you have done. And we are so thankful you were there when the accident happened."

Dr. Watson shook the extended hand. "Glad I was there to help. It seems like God puts us exactly where we need to be at just the right time." He patted the woman's soft hand in his.

"Jannah, you will have new chores now." Dr. Watson squatted down next to the child. "Tucker is ready to spend some time outside, but you must keep him on a leash and not let him run too much yet. You can walk him around your block a twice a day. When you bring him back in two weeks, we will see if he is ready to go without a leash. Sound like a plan?"

"Oh! Tucker will love being outside again!" Jannah squealed and wrapped her arms around the doctor's neck.

"You go make sure Tucker's leash is on tight, and I will explain the new dressing changes to your mom."

Dr. Watson turned to Marta after the door shut. "You did do a first-class job with Tucker's wound care, you know. It will be much easier now with the stitches out—just change the dressing every other day, unless it gets wet."

"I can do that." Marta nodded, listening to the instructions. Her voice lowered, and her brow furrowed as she continued, "I know the bill is going to be pretty high. I was wondering if—"

Dr. Watson interrupted. "About the bill," he said, "it has been taken care of for you. All past and future care for Tucker has been covered."

Marta's jaw dropped, and her eyes narrowed. She stammered, "Wha—what? How? Who?"

"I cannot tell you." Dr. Watson crossed his arms over his chest. "All I can tell you is that it has been paid."

"I-I don't understand," Marta stuttered. "Why would someone pay my vet bill? And why can't you tell me who did it?"

"The bill was paid with a cashier's check," Pat answered. "Obviously, there are people in your world who think very much of you and Jannah, and one of them wanted to help this way."

"It must have been James." Marta turned her back to Dr. Watson and muttered quietly, "That is just the kind of thing he would do for us."

Dr. Watson touched Marta's elbow and tugged to turn her back to him. The uncertainty in her eyes made his heart squeeze. "Well, I promised to keep the secret, and I cannot confirm if it was James or someone else. It has been my pleasure to deliver the news." His eye caught sight of Jannah in the office doorway. "Looks like Jannah and Tucker are ready to go! We will see you again in two weeks, okay?"

CHAPTER SIX

DONNA GRABBED A JACKET AND headed out the door for her afternoon walk. After a few minutes, she tied the jacket sleeves around her waist. The day was warming up, and the weather was delightful. Donna's walk led her to the neighborhood's park, where she liked to sit to soak up the sunshine and watch the children play.

She breathed in the fresh air, and it awakened every cell in her body. She pushed a strand of hair behind her ear. The recent trim flattered the shape of her face. It had been a *long* time since she last felt pretty. The ugliness of her soul's misery had drained her body of any beauty. But her newfound inner peace radiated to her face, and the smiles she extended to others were returned every time.

Her park bench was empty this afternoon. The young mothers were there, but they were busy pushing kids in swings or holding small hands of children swooping down slides. The mothers intrigued Donna. She watched them breathlessly, as if in expectation of a happy ending to a movie. Their smiling faces and noisy chatter thrilled her.

A dog barked across the park, startling Donna. A young boy was being pulled along by an energetic dog on a leash. A smile washed across her face as she imagined little Jannah with her beloved Tucker tugging against his leash. James had shared the news of Tucker's accident, and he had kindly kept her updated on his recovery.

James kept her updated on many aspects of Jannah and Marta's lives. He sent pictures of birthdays, school programs, and Christmases. Each picture brought her so much joy. She poured over them, memorizing the freckles on the faces of her daughter and granddaughter. Donna wanted to beg James to introduce them. She was so eager to meet the two people who had unknowingly transformed her life. But she had no right, and that fact silenced her longings.

Still, she often imagined what it would be like to face Marta. Would her daughter ever understand why Donna had to place her for adoption? Could a mother-daughter relationship be built without the foundation of childhood? Indeed, would Marta even want a relationship with her? Perhaps it would be best to keep her distance and be content with the updates James funneled to her.

Donna tucked those thoughts away and stood to start for home. Before she felt steady on her feet, pain ripped through her head, and she grasped for the bench. The intense pain knocked the breath out of her. Donna's knees buckled, and she fell to the ground, instinctively curling into a ball as she clutched her pounding head. She opened her mouth to shout for help, but blackness swallowed her words.

LIGHT PRICKED BEHIND DONNA'S EYES. She couldn't open her eyes, but she felt straps tighten around her waist and heard doors slam. There was a chaos of voices surrounding her. They were talking about Donna. What was wrong with her? Why couldn't she speak? Her head still ached. Horrible cramps surged through her body. If she had a voice, she would have wailed in misery. She could never remember hurting like this.

She was vaguely aware of movement, being pulled from the ambulance, and pushed down hallways. Donna still couldn't open her eyes, and she felt dizzy.

Please, just stop, and make the pain go away, she begged silently.

Cool monitors were attached to her chest. A blood pressure cuff tightened on her arm—tighter and tighter, until she wanted to scream. She wished she could scream. They kept talking about her as if she couldn't hear. No one knew her name. She did not carry her wallet during her walks, so there was no way for them to ID her, check her medical history, or notify any friends or family.

But all of Donna's thoughts and worries melted away as her pain subsided. She relaxed into the warm blankets and sank into a silent sleep.

CHAPTER SEVEN

DR. JOHN WRIGHT SHUFFLED THROUGH the stack of papers littered with sticky notes demanding his signature. He disliked this part of his job more and more every day. Indeed, retiring grew more and more tempting. The hospital board was already searching for his replacement, but few applicants were qualified for his position. John had privately vowed to maintain his position at the hospital until a new doctor committed to the board. His thoughts were interrupted by a soft knock at the door.

"Dr. Wright, you are needed in the ER," the young woman said. "They have a Jane Doe who appears to have suffered a stroke."

John looked up from his work, and a weary sigh escaped his lips. "I was about to finish for the day and head home. Is no other doctor available?"

"I'm not sure." She shrugged. "The nurse did ask for you specifically, but I can check to see what other doctors are available."

"No. I will head that way." He pushed back from his desk and grabbed his white coat.

Inside the emergency room, John scrubbed his hands and slipped behind the curtain to take inventory of the staff at the bedside. It was a capable crew. He glanced at the face of the woman on the stretcher, and he slapped his chest as he gasped. She was no Jane Doe!

"Dr. Wright!" a nurse exclaimed. "Is there something wrong? Do you know this woman?"

John shouldered closer to the stretcher without answering. He sucked in a deep breath as he searched the woman's face to make sure he was not mistaken. It was her.

"Do you know this woman?" the nurse repeated.

"I do," John whispered. "She was my first wife."

The nurse looked around the room at the others on the team. There was surprise on every face. "Do you want me to call in another doctor?"

"No," John answered without hesitation. "Get me her latest vitals and the exact time of the ambulance dispatch. Let's get a CT scan going. And make sure the thrombo injection is available." He paused in his rapid orders, his heart still pounding at the sight of Donna on the stretcher.

"She had no identifying information with her," the nurse explained. "Do you know who we should contact?"

John's eyes studied the vitals report. "I will call the children as soon as I can step away. For now, we need to get her stabilized." He searched Donna's face for signs of facial slump. If only she were conscious, he could evaluate her speech and movement. He placed a hand on Donna's shoulder and leaned closer.

"Donna, can you hear me? This is John, and I need to ask you some questions if you can hear me." John handed the chart to the nurse beside him as he watched for any response.

Donna's eyes fluttered open and darted from face to face, towering over her. Her eyes begged for understanding of her voiceless pleas.

"Donna!" he gasped. "Can you hear me?" Donna closed and opened her eyes. Was she trying to respond? John noted the panic in her short breaths, panting like a caged animal pressing against his bars. Many of his stroke patients described the sensation of being unable to communicate like struggling to breathe and suffocating from the effort.

"Can you move your arm?" he asked. Donna slowly jerked her hand to reach for him, indicating little control.

"Do you remember what happened?" he quizzed further.

Donna's lips moved, but no words came out. Then she clamped her mouth shut.

"It's okay," John encouraged her. "Don't get frustrated yet. It appears you have suffered a stroke. We are going to give you an injection to break up any blood clots and speed your recovery." He patted her hand and turned to review the information gathered by the EMTs. Time was in their favor. The injection would be administered well within the three-hour window to maximize the chances for the least disability.

John gave orders to have Donna prepped. As with many medical procedures, one possible outcome of the injection would be death. That fact had never felt so significant to John. He had done enough in the past to make this woman's existence miserable. Now, her very life was in his hands.

As a nurse placed the syringe in his hands, John's medical training took control. "There will be a brief sting," he explained. He withdrew the needle and observed his patient for any immediate side effects. His free hand patted Donna's arm.

The touch drummed up memories of his previous life as her husband. They had met when he was in medical school. Donna was the bookstore clerk who had checked out his purchases for a semester's classes. Her timid beauty had caught his eye, and he teased her for taking all his money. A few years later, they laughed together about that line, joking about how she had continued to take all his money as his wife. In truth, Donna had asked little of him—as a husband or in the divorce proceedings. The guilt that ate at him prompted his generosity in the settlement. She had never mistreated him and had worked long hours to help cover living expenses while he finished his schooling.

His thoughts jerked back to reality when Donna struggled to move her arm from his touch. It was a slow movement, delayed by stroke effects or by hesitancy to be so familiar. He looked up and found her eyes fixed on him. They glistened with moisture. Was she crying? Her facial expressions were speaking for her. John dealt with stroke victims enough to recognize their frustration when communication was hindered. Understanding became a guessing game.

John rested his other hand on top of Donna's. "You need to rest now, Donna," he said. "We will contact your regular doctor and let him know you are here." He stood to leave. "And I will call the children—if that's okay with you?" Donna blinked her eyes. John knew it was all she could do.

CHAPTER EIGHT

JAMES SMOOTHED HIS WHITE HAIR into place as he grabbed a jacket. The trip to visit Donna would be a day-long adventure, so he pulled a couple snack cakes from the pantry and shoved them in his pocket. A thermos of coffee would tide him over until he stopped somewhere for gas.

Donna hadn't answered when he called her last night to remind her of their visit. James thought nothing of it, though, because Donna had told him she sometimes walked a few blocks in the evenings. He had meant to call her again, but it was far too late when he finally remembered. The visit had been planned for several weeks. Surely, Donna would remember he was coming.

He grabbed the folder of pictures he had been gathering to share with Donna. She would be pleased to see Tucker was doing well and running outside again. James had snapped a few pictures of the dog and Jannah playing together in the grass. There were also a couple candid pictures of Marta. He had to take them secretly because he hadn't told Marta he was keeping Donna updated on the happenings in her life. A heavy sigh pressed into his chest at the thought. He needed to talk to Marta about her biological mother, and he would. Sometime.

James flipped on his favorite radio channel as he drove out of town. They were having a lively political discussion again, so he switched it off after a few minutes. There were enough things going on in his own life to keep his thoughts busy. The staged radio debate only cluttered his mind. The quiet hum of the engine below him was a welcome reprieve.

He remembered when Jannah asked him why her mother was always so sad. He was still trying to sort out the answer. The grief process is different for everyone. James had learned that fact during his years of pastoring. His first reaction was to assume Marta was still grieving the deaths of her husband and stepson. That would not be unreasonable. Her son's accident and husband's suicide had occurred in such a short time span. But the longer he thought, he began to wonder if something else was bothering Marta. Maybe he needed to just ask Marta!

Maybe he could also ask her about the man he saw visiting her house. It wasn't really his business, but James was positive the man at Marta's door was the young veterinarian who had helped Tucker. The first time he visited, James watched Marta call Tucker outside to the front deck. James excused that visit. It wasn't unheard of for a veterinarian to follow up on such severe wounds. But the vet returned several times. James bit his lower lip and tilted his head as he mulled over the possibilities.

Thoughts of Donna also swirled in his head. She had asked on their last phone call if she could meet her daughter and granddaughter sometime. He hadn't known what to say! Marta had never expressed interest in meeting her biological mother. Donna's request was timid and humble. James was stuck in the middle and struggled with the inequity of their situation. He had complete access to the daughter he had relinquished at birth, but Donna never saw her again after signing the papers at the hospital. James wanted Donna to have the same opportunity, but it wasn't his to give.

Frustrated with a lack of resolutions, James switched on the radio and scanned through stations until he found some music. It wasn't his kind of music, but it did distract his mind. After several hours, he arrived at Donna's house. A car was in the driveway. He assumed Donna had a car but had never asked about it. She had probably forgotten to pull it into the garage after running errands.

James grabbed the pictures and headed to the door. He glanced around Donna's yard. Unlike the first time he had visited, the lawn was well-maintained, and colorful flowers peeked up at him from different spots in the yard. The life changes Donna had experienced were evidenced in her yard alone. A smile tugged at James' lips as he rang the doorbell.

The door swung open, and a stranger stood there. Or had he seen the young woman before? There was something quite familiar about her.

"May I help you?" she asked.

"Oh!" James stammered. "I was looking for Donna. Is she home?"

A puzzled look crossed the woman's face. "No, she's not here. Who is asking for her?"

"I am an old friend of Donna's," James replied. "We had plans to eat lunch together today. I tried calling her last night, but there was no answer."

"She'll be sorry she missed you." She cocked an eyebrow as she continued, "You didn't tell me your name."

"James. James Hawthorne. We went to high school together," James explained.

"Well, James, I assume you don't know my mother suffered a stroke and has been recuperating at a nursing home here in town. She will be discharged in about a week, so I came over today to make sure the house was tidied up before she gets home."

"Oh, no!" Breath left his lungs in a rush. That would explain why there had been no word from Donna for several weeks. "I am so sorry to hear that! No, I did not know."

"She has been at the nursing home for almost two months," the daughter said. "She is very anxious to get home, and I think she will do well here. She has made a lot of progress."

"I am glad to hear that!" The panic in his heart calmed a little.

The daughter held out her hand to James. "I guess I haven't introduced myself," she said. "I am Donna's daughter, Elizabeth."

James shook the hand offered to him. That's why she looked familiar. Donna had pictures of Elizabeth on her mantel. "It is nice to meet you, Elizabeth. Do you think your mother would be up for a visitor at the nursing home?"

"Oh, certainly!" Elizabeth answered as she turned to grab a notepad off the foyer table behind her. "Let me write down the address for you. The nursing home is right on the highway on the east side of town. You can't miss it. She is in Room 102." She tore the page from the pad and handed it to James.

"Thank you." James glanced at the address and tucked the paper in his shirt pocket. His gaze quickly roamed Elizabeth's face. There was a definite resemblance between her and Marta. Was it their smiles?

Elizabeth crossed her arms and leaned against the door frame. "I am sure she will be glad to see you, but it is difficult for her to speak," she cautioned. "If you give her time, she will eventually get the words out."

James stepped back. "Thank you, again. And it was nice to meet you, Elizabeth."

"Likewise."

James waved as he turned and hurried back to his car. He sank down into the seat and gripped the steering wheel. It had never occurred to him that Donna might have had some kind of medical emergency. What if she had died? No one would have known to notify him.

A few minutes later, James pulled into the parking lot of the nursing home. As a minister, he made many calls on parishioners who resided at nursing homes. Still, the setting never made him feel comfortable. The display of frail humanity was overwhelming every time. He took a deep breath before stepping out of the car. His steps were heavy as he headed toward the entrance.

Inside, the residents were gathering for lunch. Some were being pushed in wheelchairs into the dining room. Others were struggling independently toward their meals. The noisy chatter of residents greeting each other made James feel like an outsider. Coming here was not a good idea, or at least, the timing was not good. As he turned to go, a woman touched his arm.

"Can I help you find someone?"

James started at her voice. "I was looking for Donna Wright, but I see I've come at an inconvenient time," he replied.

"Not at all," the woman countered. "Donna usually takes her meals in her room. I would be glad to show you the way. And I could order a lunch tray for you, if you'd like."

The woman's broad smile put James at ease. "Do you think she will mind having a visitor while she eats?"

"I don't think she will mind at all." She waved him down the hall. "Follow me. Her room is this way."

James quickened his pace to keep up. Minus the occasional empty wheelchairs, the hallway was inviting. Elegantly framed pictures and seasonal décor brought life to the space. The woman paused before entering the last room.

"May I tell Donna who is here to see her?"

"James."

"I will be right back," the woman said as she slipped inside the door.

In a matter of seconds, she returned and held the door open. "Donna is very pleased you have come to see her. Just dial one on the phone if you want a lunch tray. Enjoy your visit!"

Donna was seated in a wheelchair at a small table near the large window in her room. James sucked in a deep breath as he glanced at the minimal furnishings: a facility bed and simple nightstand. There were no touches of home.

James hoped Donna wouldn't notice the forced cheer in his voice. "Hi, Donna! Do you mind if we visit while you eat?"

A smile wobbled across her face. "Welcome," she whispered.

James sat down on the folding chair the nurse had set next to the table. He sent up a silent prayer. *God, help me to say the right thing.*

"How did you find me?" She struggled over every word.

"I went to your house. We had planned to eat lunch together today, remember?" James waited for her response.

Donna shook her head. "Sorry."

"That's okay." James touched her arm. "Elizabeth was at your house, and she told me you were here."

"Lizzie?" Donna asked. "Why was she there?"

"She said you will be coming home soon, and she wanted everything to be ready for you."

Donna put down her fork and swiped at her mouth with a napkin. She pushed her tray away from her.

"Please go ahead and eat." James hated for her to skip lunch on account of him. "Or would you rather I come back later?"

"Not hungry." She swallowed with concentrated effort, laying the napkin on the table. "Want to visit."

"It sounds like you will be going home soon, then?"

"Not soon enough."

"Can you tell me what happened?"

"Stroke at the park." She licked her lips between words as if moistening them would make speaking easier.

"Someone at the park called for help?" James pieced the puzzle together.

She nodded. "Don't remember after that."

"I wish I had known," James told her. "I would have come to visit you sooner."

"Didn't have my phone." She averted her eyes and picked at the napkin on her tray. "Didn't know your number."

James bit his tongue. What a burden for Donna to bear. He hadn't intended to scold her. Of course, her family didn't know to contact him. How would she explain their relationship, after all? Could she say he was the father of her child no one else knew existed? Hardly!

"Well, I'm here now." James smiled, reached into his pocket, and spread the pictures on the table. "I brought some pictures for you."

Donna's fingers fumbled with a picture of Marta. A sigh of frustration escaped her lips, making James' heart clench for her. He picked it up and handed it to her.

"That's a good picture of her, isn't it?" It was one of his favorites of Marta. It captured his daughter's beauty in a rare relaxed moment as she sat on the front porch, the breeze teasing her hair.

Donna was silent as she studied the face in the picture. "Thought I would die and never see her." Her voice faltered between words.

The unfairness of her situation pricked at James' emotions. "Maybe it will happen sometime," he encouraged. James reached for the picture of Jannah and Tucker. "Tucker is getting along very well now," he remarked, hoping to lighten the conversation.

"Good!"

"Marta told me someone paid Tucker's veterinary bill. In full. She was very surprised." James watched Donna closely. Maybe she was the mysterious donor!

She only nodded. But did James imagine a smile at the corners of her mouth?

"The veterinarian wouldn't say who paid," James continued, hoping to pry out her admission of benevolence. "The bill was a big concern for Marta. It was an answer to *my* prayers to have it covered for her!" He paused. "I assured Marta it wasn't me. But she cannot imagine who else would have done such a thing."

James never moved his eyes from Donna. Her expression revealed nothing. She simply looked pleased someone had been so kind to Marta.

Certain the benefactor was still unidentified, James handed another picture to Donna. Her gaze roamed over it for several long moments. It was a picture of Marta and Jannah together.

"Look alike," Donna assessed as she handed the picture back to James.

"They do! And Marta looks like you in many ways."

"Want to see her." Donna's head sank, and moisture gathered between her eyelashes.

"I know. Do you want to contact her and see how she responds?"

Donna nodded her head. "Before it is too late."

James took a pen from the table and wrote Marta's address on the empty envelope. He did not have Marta's permission for this, but it felt like the right thing to do, anyway. He gathered the pictures, tucking them back into the envelope and scooting it toward Donna's hand.

"I'm going to head home." James pushed his chair back from the table. "I'm so relieved I met Elizabeth, and she told me where to find you. I would've been worried sick." Donna fumbled with the envelope and pressed it close to her chest. "The next time we talk, you will be home again. I'll be praying everything goes well and you make progress every day!"

"Thank you, James." Donna turned her head away to hide the tears. "And thank you for the pictures."

CHAPTER NINE

MARTA GLANCED AROUND THE LIVING room one last time. It looked perfect. Everything was in its place. She had worked for days, cleaning and organizing every room. Was she really going through with this? The gravity of her desperation exhausted her.

Scheduling this appointment without rousing James' or Jannah's suspicions was quite difficult. She had wrestled with the idea of confiding in James, but he would attempt to fix things for her. Marta would not let him jeopardize his own financial stability trying to solve her dilemma.

Marta paused at the kitchen window as the realtor's car pulled into the driveway. She sucked in a weary breath and headed to answer the doorbell. It was the right thing to do—the only thing to do, really.

"Good afternoon, Mrs. Newton. I am Bill Getty with Preferred Properties." The realtor's perky greeting chafed against Marta's reluctance. She shook his hand out of obligation.

"Hello. Come in."

"This is a well-maintained property," Bill assessed as he stepped into the front room. "I could tell when I pulled into the driveway. Let's take a look around, and then we can talk about the listing process."

"Certainly," Marta agreed. She led the way to the kitchen, walking slowly to accommodate his note-taking.

"Would you be interested in including the kitchen appliances in the listing? That sometimes makes the deal."

Marta opened her mouth to reply, but no words came. There were so many details she hadn't even considered. "Well, I guess that would work," she finally answered. "I have no idea if these appliances would fit wherever I would move, anyway."

"You can think about it and let me know later," Bill replied. "If you decide to include them, I would need to know their approximate purchase dates."

"Okay," Marta said. She suppressed an overwhelmed sigh.

"Let's take a look at the bedrooms now," Bill directed. "I believe you told us there are four?"

"Technically there are four. We use the smallest room for an office."

"Not a problem if there is a closet and a window. We will list it as a bedroom. And there are three bathrooms?"

"Yes. One in the master bedroom, a full bath near the other bedrooms, and a half bath near the front room."

"Excellent! Let me make a note of the shower and tub combinations." He penciled more notes on his pad as they strolled into the master bedroom. "Do you mind if I look in the closets?"

"Not at all." Marta slid the door open to the closet. Two months ago, she would have cringed at the idea of a stranger opening any closet in her house. But selling was her only option. Her privacy would have to be sacrificed.

Would Bill notice the patched drywall where a bullet had lodged? Were there any visible blood stains on the floor?

Marta followed the realtor down the hallway as he inspected each bedroom. She muffled her objection when he stepped across the threshold into the privacy of Jannah's room. She turned her back, focusing on Jannah's beloved pile of stuffed animals.

"Mrs. Newton?" Bill's voice jerked her back to reality.

"Oh, I'm sorry." Marta shook her head. "I didn't hear what you said."

"I asked if you plan to leave the ceiling fans in all the bedrooms?"

Plan? Marta hadn't planned any of this! Having a stranger walking through her house, poking into the private spaces of her heart was the *last* thing she would have *planned* to do. "The fans can stay," she finally replied.

"Can we look at the furnace and water heater?"

"Of course. Those are in the basement." Marta opened the door to the basement and flipped the light switch.

"I will also need to know the age of both of these," Bill said as he took note of the brand and size of the equipment. "Central air is attached, I assume?"

"Yes." She bit her bottom lip in concern. She wasn't sure she had all the information Bill wanted. Her husband had lived in this house several years before they married, and there had been few updates to any of the appliances since then.

The realtor stuck his pen over his ear and tucked his notepad under his arm. "Let's go out to the deck and take a look outside," Bill said.

Ah, the deck! The sacred place she had spent hours tending her flowers and mending her heart after the death of her husband! Marta led him to the deck, her mood sinking deeper with every step.

"Such a private backyard!" Bill exclaimed, observing the colorful flower pots tucked around the cushioned outdoor chairs. "It almost feels like you don't have neighbors!" He pulled the pen from his ear and jotted another note on his pad. "Speaking of neighbors, do you have any concerns about the current residents of the neighborhood?"

Marta shook her head. "No concerns at all. We are very fortunate to have wonderful neighbors." She was speaking of one neighbor in particular. There were no words to describe how Marta dreaded telling that one neighbor of her plans to move.

"Excellent!" Bill replied. "I'll need some information about the siding and roof before we can list, but you can get back to me about that along with the other things I've detailed. Let's go inside, and I can explain how our agency's listing will work. I would also like to take some pictures we can include in the online listing, if you decide to go that route."

They settled down at the dining room table, and Bill spread out several forms to be completed. Marta kept an eye on the clock while the realtor progressed through the stack of papers. She hoped James and Jannah would not return from the dog park until all this business was done. Marta scribbled her signature on form after form.

Finally, Bill gathered the papers into two piles, one for himself and one for Marta. "Don't hesitate to call me if you have any other questions," he said. "Get me that info, and I will have the listing ready to go! You have a really nice home that should sell in a short time." He stood and offered another handshake. The easy part was done. Now, she would have to devise a way to tell Jannah and James—before the realtor's sign was posted in her yard.

"BUT *WHY*, MOM?" JANNAH'S VOICE cracked.

"I think it will be best." The answer was lame and inadequate. How could she help her daughter understand their financial situation after her father had committed suicide?

"But what about Grandpa Hawkeye?" Jannah hugged Tucker's neck, burying her face. "He will be so sad if we move away!"

"I know, honey," Marta assured. "He can come visit us."

"Where are we going?"

"I don't know yet." Marta struggled to hold her composure under the onslaught of questions. "We can't make that decision until we get this house sold."

"Are we going to another town?"

"No," Marta reassured. "You go to school here, and my job is here. We will not be moving to another town, I promise."

"Then why do we have to move at all?"

The conversation had gone full circle, and Marta didn't have the strength to go through it all a second time. "I am sorry, Jannah." She sighed. "We sometimes have to do things we don't want to do."

"Well, *you* are going to have to tell Grandpa Hawkeye, and he will *not* be happy about this either!" Jannah jumped up and ran to the front door. "Come on, Tucker! Let's go outside." The door slammed hard behind them.

Marta stood at the window, watching. Jannah's back was to her, but her small shoulders heaved with sobs. Marta's heart twisted. How many more times did her daughter have to suffer? She collapsed into a chair. How would she ever tell James the news?

"I SIGNED THE LISTING AGREEMENT yesterday."

Marta and James sipped their coffee at the kitchen bar. He set down his cup and rested his chin on his clasped hands. Marta could not look at him. There was no need. She knew his heart was breaking.

"Did you consider refinancing?" James asked softly.

"Of course," Marta replied. "Even at the lower payment, I would not have been able to make it work."

"I would have helped."

A tear formed, blurring Marta's vision. "I know, but I cannot ask that of you."

"You wouldn't have had to *ask*. I would have done it without a thought!" Now, his voice cracked with the heaviness of the news.

"I know. But I couldn't allow you to stretch your own finances."

James looked into her eyes. "Have you told Jannah?"

"Yes, and she is very upset," Marta replied. "She's equally as upset about how you will take the news as she is about moving. She loves you very much."

James looked away and released a deep sigh. "I love her very much, too. And I love *you* very much. I wish there was some other way to solve this problem!"

"So do I," Marta responded, "but it seems this is our only option."

James reached to gather Marta's hand in his. He patted her soft skin with his aged palm. How he wished he could have had the opportunity to father his daughter as a child, when he could have easily provided answers for her needs. Now, the need she had was well beyond his means, and his heart wept at the thought. But this was his opportunity to demonstrate to his daughter the goodness of her God. He could ask God to provide some solution to Marta's situation without having to sell her home. If that wasn't God's plan for Marta, James would pray for peace for all three of them—Marta, Jannah, and himself. Surely, God would not separate them now when they had just found each other!

James stood at the window, watching helplessly as the realtor pounded a stake into Marta's yard. The thud of every pound rang in James' ears until he wanted to scream. Was Jannah watching from her own window? He ached for her and Marta.

His brain was exhausted. He'd spent the last hours mentally racing through alternatives. He had offered to move Marta and Jannah into his own home. It was spacious, and he would be overjoyed to have them. But Marta had declined, pointing out it was her responsibility to provide for Jannah. James wanted to plead, but it wasn't his place to tell Marta what to do. She was a capable adult and had made decisions without his advice for many years.

At last, the pounding stopped, and the "For Sale" sign was in place. Would the property sell quickly, or would Marta's financial strain continue for months?

The realtor was packing up his tools when a brown Jeep pulled onto the curb in front of their house. James sighed as Dr. Watson jumped out. Had Marta shared the news with him?

The doctor stopped to visit with the realtor. James could only imagine the questions being asked. A handshake later, Dr. Watson continued toward the front door. Before he rang the doorbell, Tucker and Jannah burst out to greet him. Tucker barked in excitement, and his lopsided hind end wagged right along with his tail. Dr. Watson squatted, getting eye level with Tucker and rubbing between his ears. After a few moments, he retrieved a dog biscuit from his pocket.

Marta joined them on the front porch. Subtle hints over the last several weeks suggested Marta and Dr. Watson were forming a friendship beyond veterinarian and client. Judging from his own interactions with the doctor, James was ready to give his approval. He stepped away from the window to give them privacy.

CHAPTER TEN

PAT WAITED TO SPEAK UNTIL Jannah and Tucker ran off to play Frisbee in the yard. "So, what's up with the 'For Sale' sign?"

Marta sucked in a deep breath, averting her eyes. "I decided to list the house. It's too much for me to keep up. We are going to look for something smaller."

"Oh." Pat forced himself to focus on the lively game in the front yard. As the three-legged dog ran after the Frisbee, Pat cheered, "Go, Tucker! Get it before Jannah does!" He cleared his throat and turned back to Marta. "I hope you aren't planning to move out of the community."

"No. My job is here, and Jannah would refuse to move to a different school." She shook her head and a half-smile tugged at her cheeks. "She would refuse to move at all if she thought she could get away with it."

"Well, I'm glad to hear that! I am pretty handy with a hammer and know a few things about plumbing and electricity," Pat added, "if there are things I could do to keep you here."

Marta smiled, but her words were forced. "Oh, it's a lot of things— you know, keeping the appliances running, the bushes trimmed, the house painted . . . "

"And the bills paid?"

Marta averted her eyes again. "Mostly, it's the upkeep that is overwhelming."

"Well, don't forget my offer to help," Pat replied. "Here, or wherever you happen to move."

"You are a wonderful friend. But I could not impose on you."

56

"No imposition! I need to keep an eye on the amputee, anyway." Pat grinned, thankful for his convenient excuse to continue dropping by Marta's house.

A soft laugh bubbled up from Marta. "You have spoiled Tucker, bringing him dog treats every time you come!"

"I can't give my clients lollipops now, can I?" Pat teased. He tore his gaze away from Marta's face, forcing his attention to the dog again. "Tucker is doing so well. At the accident, I knew Tucker would have all he needed to recover. Jannah talked so softly to him. It's obvious how much she loves him."

"They are inseparable," Marta agreed. "I think about how differently that day could have ended if you weren't there."

Pat glanced at Marta in time to watch a gentle shudder pass across her shoulders. "I'm glad I was there." Pat was certain he hadn't just saved Tucker that day. He also saved the happiness of two people who had assumed an important place in his heart—a place he vowed no woman would ever go. Still, Marta was there, always a breath away from his awareness, in his last thoughts before he drifted off to sleep and often a mirage he chased in his dreams.

CHAPTER ELEVEN

DONNA WAITED FOR HER DAUGHTER to arrive. It was discharge day, and she was impatient to get back to her own surroundings. Life would not be as simple anymore, but she was determined to make it work. She had passed all the occupational therapy tests and was given a checklist of things to change around her house.

The safety precautions were drilled into her head. Meals would be delivered; a housekeeper would tend her home; and even a nurse would make house calls. Still, Elizabeth had agreed to stay until Donna felt comfortable being home alone.

Overall, the residual effects of her stroke were minor. Speech was a work-in-progress, and she used a cane to walk. She had graduated from the walker, and she was so relieved! Clinging to a walker made her remember the purposeless time in her life she wished to forget. Donna prayed she wouldn't have to depend on a walker ever again.

Yes, she had done a lot of praying while she was confined to the nursing home. She prayed for strength and thanked God for the mothers at the park who had called for help. She thanked God for her ex-husband's wisdom in treating her at the hospital. She thanked God for bringing James Hawthorne back into her life. She prayed for her children—all of them.

Donna had tucked the envelope of pictures and Marta's home address into her purse. Just knowing where she lived gave her peace. She spent so many years agonizing over what had happened to the child she had placed for adoption. Now, she had a physical address for Marta, and it felt like a lifeline!

Donna had mentally composed a letter to Marta but never committed it to paper. Worry that her secret would be compromised had stopped her. But the need to make amends with Marta slowly outweighed her fear. A handwritten letter would be difficult to manage physically and, even more difficult, emotionally. Donna wracked her brain for a way to reach out to her long-lost daughter.

"There you are!" Elizabeth's greeting startled Donna back to reality. "I have the car out front. I'll load up your things before we get you checked out."

"Glad to see you." Donna's tongue felt awkward against her lips. The words were so clear in her head. Why was it such a struggle to say them?

"Are you ready to go?" Elizabeth sat down on the edge of the bed near Donna's wheelchair.

"Yes!" Her answer was strong and quick. Going home was the motivation for every task the last few weeks.

"Let's get busy then!" Elizabeth stood and began to pull hangers from the closet.

Donna watched her daughter pack up her few belongings. Elizabeth folded the clothing into a suitcase and placed a comb, toiletries, and Donna's purse into a packing box.

How fortunate for Donna her daughter was not tied down to a job. With a dentist for a husband, Elizabeth didn't need to work. She was content to stay at home and care for their daughter. While Elizabeth was caring for Donna, her mother-in-law was able to see her granddaughter off to school and escort her to activities. Still, Donna sensed Elizabeth was anxious to get her mother settled in so she could return to her home as well.

Donna couldn't help but wonder how she would react to the news about Marta. If Donna pursued a relationship with Marta, her other children would have to know. She imagined the boys would shrug it off easier than Elizabeth. Would Elizabeth feel displaced or threatened by the reality of another daughter? A deep sigh escaped Donna's chest, stirring Elizabeth's notice.

"Why such a big sigh?" Elizabeth zipped the suitcase and set it down on the rollers before cocking a curious look at her mother.

Donna's attention jerked back to her daughter. "Just tired," she excused herself.

"We will have you home and into bed in no time."

"Sounds good," Donna agreed. The bed beside her looked inviting, but the quiet solitude of her home compelled her heart.

"I think we have everything." Elizabeth glanced around the room to make sure they weren't leaving anything behind. "Let's go sign the discharge papers and get on the road!" She loaded the suitcase and box onto the cart and pushed it out into the hallway.

The discharge paperwork was waiting for them at the nurses' station. Elizabeth studied the medicine list and made note of two prescriptions she would need to have filled. She initialed the safety instructions and signed several forms to wrap up Donna's stay.

One aide rolled the cart to the front door while another helped Donna into the car. Transferring from the wheelchair into the car's seat was a complicated procedure. Leaving her home would take so much effort. Dread reached up and gripped her heart. She would become a prisoner within her home's walls again.

Donna had feared those dark thoughts would visit her. She prayed for her physical strength to return and for a positive attitude in the meantime. The depression that held her captive in the past loomed over her like a mocking shadow. Donna was determined not to succumb to it again.

She breathed in, enjoying the fresh air. The comforts of home would be so wonderful, but she worried about the medical team she was leaving behind. They had all worked so hard to help her progress and had cheered her on when she wanted to quit. Could she exercise and make good choices without them? Now, there would be no warm meals appearing on a regular schedule and no aide folding her laundry. When Elizabeth returned home, Donna would truly be on her own. The dread in her spirit reared its ugly head again.

DONNA SANK INTO HER LIFT chair, exhausted from the effort of dressing for the meeting with the home health care coordinator. The nursing home staff had arranged the meeting, assuring Donna the extra help at her home would be beneficial.

Elizabeth answered the door and led the visitor to the front room. The perky, young woman offered her hand to Donna.

"Hi, Donna! My name is Sharon. I'm a nurse with the home health office here in town. I bet you are glad to be home!"

The meeting was a blur. In a matter of minutes, Sharon had scheduled nursing and home aide visits. People would come all through the week to help with chores, meals, bathing, medications, and check-ins. She even arranged for an alert system to be installed and divvied out prescriptions into her medicine box. She put emergency contacts numbers up on Donna's refrigerator and toured her home to make sure the bathroom and bedroom were fully accessible. At last, Sharon gathered her supplies, promising to return the next day to introduce the homemaker.

As soon as the door closed behind the nurse, Elizabeth slipped off Donna's shoes and helped her onto her bed for a nap. "Sharon seems like a very nice person, don't you think?" She pulled a light blanket over her mother.

"Yes, but not easy to have so much intrusion."

Elizabeth patted her mother's arm and tucked it under the blanket. "The help will be good for you," she encouraged. "When you feel up to taking over, you can discontinue the service. You did not agree to the help forever."

Donna nodded her head. She watched her daughter fold clothes. Elizabeth handled the clothing tenderly, placing them into the drawers exactly the way Donna would have done it herself.

"Thank you," Donna whispered.

"Oh, Mom!" Elizabeth put her hands on her hips and clicked her tongue. "I'm just glad I have been able to help you. But my time here is in jeopardy—anyone can see you are improving every day! It won't be long before you are doing all these things yourself again."

"Hope so."

Elizabeth squatted down beside her mother's bed and tucked Donna's hair behind her ear. "Anything you need before I run to the grocery store?"

"No. Go ahead."

With a few breaths, she succumbed to sleep.

CHAPTER TWELVE

JAMES TOOK ONE LAST LOOK around the kitchen before heading to the garage. Everything was as it should be. No water dripping at the sink or from the refrigerator door. Toaster unplugged. It had been his wife's routine when leaving home on a trip. Today, he planned to visit Donna. They had talked on the phone a few days ago, and he was encouraged by how strong her voice sounded. Hopefully, strength was returning to her body as well.

The "For Sale" sign in Marta's yard jeered at him as he pulled away from his house. Marta had shared that there was one couple who had looked at the property a second time and seemed interested in making an offer, but there was nothing in writing yet. James dreaded hearing about an official offer. His physical proximity to his daughter and granddaughter would end, and his heart ached at the thought.

Once away from city traffic, James' mind got to work. How much of Marta's situation should he share with Donna? Of course, Donna would ask about her. He didn't want to give Donna more to worry about, but he doubted he could even mention Marta's name without the new concern betraying his attempt to spare Donna.

Should he tell Donna about how Dr. Watson was showing up at Marta's more and more often? The whole family seemed drawn to the doctor. There was no mistaking Tucker and Pat had formed a lasting relationship during the dog's recovery, and that alone endeared Pat to little Jannah! As for himself, James had only good things to say about the man and found no reason to discourage his blooming friendship with Marta.

James drove several miles as "what-ifs" knocked around in his head. What if Pat and Marta eventually wanted to marry? Jannah would have a daddy again, and Marta would have a husband again. Surely, Pat's income would help them keep their home.

What if Marta and Donna decided to meet? Would they feel he'd kept them apart the past few years? Would Jannah accept Donna as a grandmother? Or would Jannah keep her at arm's length and refuse to love her?

What if Donna didn't recover? What if she was running out of time to meet Marta? How would he live with the fact he had prevented Donna from enjoying Marta as a daughter?

The miles disappeared behind him as these thoughts tugged at his heart. He blew a deep sigh of relief through his lips as he pulled into Donna's driveway shortly after one o'clock. It would feel good to get out of the car and stretch his legs! He should have stopped somewhere for a sandwich, but it seemed like a waste of time. He wasn't really hungry, anyway.

There were no extra vehicles in the driveway this time, and James was relieved. Donna had not mentioned if Elizabeth had returned to her own home. Visiting with Donna alone would be easier. He would not have to be so guarded against mentioning Marta or Jannah. And their conversation would be pretty limited if those two people could not be a part of it.

He grabbed a new envelope of pictures from the passenger's seat and opened his door. Goodness! His legs felt like jelly, he had sat for so long! He glanced toward the house and found Donna standing at the door waiting for him. He waved as he approached, and a smile washed across the woman's face. She pushed the door open for him.

"Hello, James!"

"Hello, Donna!" James saw Donna was leaning on her walker. "You are up and on your feet again!" he said as the door clicked shut behind him. "It is so good to see that!"

"Still moving slowly, but moving!" She turned her walker and motioned for him to follow.

"Beautiful day for a drive," Donna said over her shoulder.

"Indeed!" James replied. "Fall is upon us, though. I can feel it in the air."

"My helper made coffee for us this morning," Donna said. "Will you pour some?"

James found a tray with two cups and saucers by the coffeemaker in the kitchen. He filled the cups, set the tray on the coffee table, and settled into the chair across from Donna's spot on the couch. He handed her one of the cups, and she cradled it in both hands to steady it.

"The heat feels good," she explained. "It is too warm to run the furnace but too chilly to sit without a blanket."

James took a sip from his cup. "I agree! And this coffee hits the spot! Thank you for thinking of it." He paused as Donna also sipped at her coffee. "How have the last few weeks gone? Your daughter has returned home now?"

"Yes, Elizabeth returned to her family. She was excellent help, but I could tell she was ready to be home." Donna's chest heaved with a heavy sigh. "I have done fine without her here, but it is very quiet again."

James smiled in understanding. "The silence can be so loud sometimes, can't it?"

"It can!" Donna agreed. "I look forward to walking again. I enjoyed the outdoors so much before the stroke."

"Judging by your progress, I think you will be outside in no time!"

"Did you bring more pictures?" Donna asked, nodding toward the envelope James had placed on the coffee table.

"I did!" James reached for the envelope and began to pull out the pictures.

"Does Marta know you are sharing pictures with me?"

James didn't raise his eyes to meet hers. He knew this question would come, and he had been dreading it. "No, I haven't told her yet.

She is dealing with some difficult issues right now. The time never seems right. I'm sorry."

Donna offered him a sad smile. "It's all right. The time needs to be right. I don't want it to be a mistake when you do tell her."

James handed the pictures to Donna, watching her face as she looked at the picture on top. It was a picture of Jannah with Tucker. The child was holding a Frisbee high in the air, and the dog was salivating with expectation. A happy smile chased away the sadness in Donna's eyes.

"It looks like Tucker has completely healed!"

"Yes, Tucker is pretty much back to normal. He has a lopsided run, but he can run! And he still is at Jannah's side if she is anywhere around."

"It also looks as if Jannah has grown five inches since the last picture I saw! She is not a little girl anymore, is she?"

A hearty laugh preceded James' answer. "No, Jannah is not a little girl anymore. She is becoming a young lady, but Tucker still brings out the kid in her."

Donna found a picture of Marta and Jannah leaning against the fender of a shiny Jeep, both sporting wide smiles. Pat knelt beside Tucker, rubbing the dog's jowls with his thumbs. "They look very happy." Donna spoke without taking her eyes off the photograph.

Happy? Were Marta and Jannah happy? This was the moment he had been contemplating. How much should he share with Donna? How much should he withhold? Was it fair for him to withhold anything?

"I think Marta and Jannah are both doing well. I hope it is not betraying Marta's trust to tell you she is struggling financially. Her husband's life insurance payout was denied because of a suicide clause. Along with considerable medical debt after the car accident, Marta is now paying all the household costs on a single salary." James sighed as he finished.

"Oh, no!" Donna responded. "That is so sad! I can only imagine how difficult it has been for Marta to make ends meet." Donna's shoulders slumped as she turned her eyes back to the picture.

"She has her house for sale now," James admitted. He shifted in his seat, crossing his arms.

"Even worse!" Donna exclaimed. "I know you have enjoyed having them so close to you. Has there been a lot of interest in the property?"

"Some. No offers yet, but a couple has come to look at it twice now."

"How does Jannah feel about moving?"

James shook his head. "She has given her mother some grief about it. But Marta has assured her they aren't moving far away."

Donna tilted her head and sighed. "But it won't be the same, will it?"

"The same as having them next door? Where I can see them every day and know they are safely home every night? Where Jannah can run over to my place anytime she wants? No, it won't be the same." James' lips pressed together in a grimace as he considered all the changes, and he felt his eyes watering.

"Is this young man in the picture the veterinarian?" Donna guessed, moving the picture closer for inspection.

Dr. Watson was a topic James was happy to discuss. "Yes, that is Dr. Watson—or Pat. He comes around fairly often. He says he is checking on Tucker, but I think it is much more than that. Jannah and Tucker are always excited to see him. But I think Marta enjoys his visits, too."

Donna's eyes narrowed before she answered. "Well, maybe the veterinarian is the solution to Marta's dilemma!"

"I won't claim I haven't thought of that," James conceded. "But I wouldn't want Marta to become involved with him because he could fix her financial problems."

"Certainly not," Donna agreed, "but if it turns out they are attracted to each other and decide to marry, perhaps the property would not need to be sold."

"Things would have to progress pretty rapidly for that to work," James cautioned. "I doubt she would decide so quickly. And I am certain she would never want Pat to feel like she married him for his money."

"Well, perhaps it will all work out, and the financial worries will go away." Donna's gaze drifted away from the picture, across the room to the family photos on her mantel. James assumed the various faces were Donna's family members.

"I met Elizabeth when I stopped here last time." James stood and walked over to the fireplace. "Can you introduce me to the other folks who keep you company in the frames there?" He turned back to Donna as the glow of a mother's pride shone on her face.

"Of course." She gleamed. "If you want to hand the pictures down to me, I can tell you a little about all of them."

James reached for the frame closest to one end of the mantel. A young man with an easy smile looked back at him.

"That's my maverick," Donna began. "He is my youngest child, and if you ask the two other children, he was spoiled. Maybe he was. Maybe he wasn't. He has had a difficult time finding his place in the world, but I know he will someday."

"His name is Maverick?" James asked.

"Oh. No, his name is Andrew. I just call him my maverick because he fits no molds. He is his own captain. But just the sound of his voice can make me smile." There was still a smile on her face as she handed the frame back to James.

James replaced the photograph and picked up the next one of a young girl who looked close to Jannah's age. He could not wait to hear the story about her!

Donna took the picture from his hands and held it close to her heart. "This is Kendra, my only grandchild so far. She is Elizabeth's daughter. She was probably five years old in this picture. Now she is eight." Donna paused. "I don't get to see her as often as I would like."

"She looks like you," James said softly.

"She looks a lot like her mother," Donna corrected. "While Elizabeth was here helping me, we talked about Kendra a lot. I wish they did not live four hours from here. I hope to be back to normal eventually, but even then, I don't think I am up to a four-hour drive by myself."

"But Elizabeth will be back to check on you. Surely, she could bring the child with her?" James' raised his eyebrows. Wasn't that a logical plan?

"She could, but now, school will be starting. And Kendra is in *everything!* She dances. She plays piano. She takes French lessons. They keep that child so busy—too busy, in my opinion."

"Does she have a dog?"

Donna chuckled. "No dog. That would be too messy for her father. He is a perfectionist. Everything has to be in its place, and dogs are seldom in their place! Before—when you first came to visit me a couple years ago—my house was never neat. I didn't have the energy to keep it up, nor did I want strangers in here cleaning it for me. Elizabeth's husband found the clutter disgusting, and I think that is one reason why he seldom comes anymore."

"I'm sorry he feels that way." James glanced around at the orderly room with well-placed decor. "But surely, that doesn't mean Kendra can't come to see you?"

"He has never said as much, but I don't think Elizabeth wants to confront him about taking Kendra away from her activities."

"Oh, how unfortunate for you!" James put the picture of her granddaughter back on the mantel. He picked up the third frame. Of another son, he guessed. "Who is this?"

"Jack is my oldest child. Well, except for Marta," Donna added. "He did exceptionally well in school, but he chose to join the navy. He is making a career of it. He will retire in a few years with a very good pension."

"Is he married?"

"No, he never did find a girl to suit him," Donna answered. "He always said the navy life wasn't the kind of life he wanted for a family. He is gone so much. I think his parents' divorce did nothing to promote marriage. It is sad he never had a family." Donna's face fell somber as she looked at her eldest son, and she handed the frame back to James.

The one remaining frame was a photo of Elizabeth. James handed the picture to Donna.

"You have already met Elizabeth," Donna reminded him.

"Yes," James agreed. "I can see from this photo that she also looks a lot like her mother."

Donna smiled. "I suppose she does. I can see some resemblance to Marta, as well. I wonder if their personalities are similar."

"Maybe someday, you will meet Marta and find out," James offered as he took the photo and replaced it on the mantel.

There were no more photos, but a nicely framed painting hung above the fireplace. "That painting is perfect for this spot." James stepped back from the mantel and cocked his head as he viewed the entire display.

"You think so?" Donna asked. "I painted it years ago."

"Really? I had no idea you are an artist!" James shifted, glancing at Donna in surprise. "It is very well done!"

"Well, thank you," Donna said. "I haven't had my paints out for many years, so I probably could not do anything even close to that quality now. It was a good distraction for me during the difficult years of my marriage. And during the divorce."

"You should get the paints out again!" James encouraged.

"Maybe I will," Donna said. "I should be able to find some room in this huge house where I could set up an easel!"

"Have Elizabeth help you set up next time she is here! And just get started!" James snapped his fingers, goading Donna with a wink.

THE AFTERNOON WITH DONNA PASSED quickly. James refilled their coffee cups, and they sat and visited until an alarm sounded, reminding Donna to take her medication. The interruption provided a good opportunity for James to get on the road. He pressed the envelope of pictures into her palm when she held it out to him. Her eyes watered with tears when they shook hands before he left.

The hum of his car broke the silence as he drove away from Donna's house. He wished he could arrange a meeting for Donna, Marta, and Jannah! Oddly enough, Donna had never asked him to do that. Nor had Marta. Perhaps it was best for him not to suggest it either. Donna just seemed lonely, and James knew getting acquainted with her first child would fill the void hovering behind her forced smiles.

It was late by the time he pulled onto his street. A soft glow of light shone from Marta's front windows, and a familiar brown Jeep was parked in the driveway. Surely, Jannah was in bed by now.

James smiled to himself as he pulled into his garage and headed for bed. Perhaps it *would* all work out, just as Donna had said.

CHAPTER THIRTEEN

MARTA TOOK A DEEP BREATH and prepared to knock on James' front door. The window was open, and he sat inside reading the newspaper. She tilted her head into his line of vision and waved. "Hey, James! Do you have a minute to talk?"

"Hi, Marta!" James grinned at her. "Come on in! Everything okay?"

Marta went inside and perched on the edge of the couch. She took another deep breath, gathering her racing thoughts. "I am not sure how this happened, but the bank called yesterday to tell me my house loan was paid off by someone who wished to remain anonymous." Marta's eyes narrowed. "You didn't do that, did you?"

"What?" James exclaimed. "No way! I wish I could have done that for you, but I could not. But I would like to thank whomever did!"

"Me, too!" Marta agreed. "If it wasn't you, it had to be Pat. He really didn't want me to move, even though I assured him I wasn't leaving the area."

"So, it's 'Pat' now?" James teased with a grin. "Well, if it was Pat, then such a gesture was very, very kind of him! Do you think he would admit it if you asked him?"

Marta shook her head. "The banker said the person wanted to remain anonymous. I am embarrassed to even ask Pat, but I can't think of anyone else who would do that for me."

"Then you don't have to move?" James wanted to be sure he understood the implications of the secret gift.

"Well, if I don't have a house payment to make, that would certainly help!" Marta answered. "There are still medical bills to pay off, but they are willing to give me time on those."

"Oh, Marta! I have been praying you wouldn't have to move. Have you told Jannah?" James threw the newspaper aside. He leaned forward with his elbows on his knees and clapped his hands in delight.

"Not yet. I wanted to know how this all happened before I said anything to her. She doesn't have to know the details, but I would sure like to know!" Confusion, laced with relief, spread across Marta's face.

"Well, I surely don't have to tell you how pleased I am!" James slapped his knees. "I know Jannah will be pleased, too!"

"Yes, she will be," Marta agreed. "But I don't think I'll be able to rest until I know who did this for us!" She shook her head before she continued. "The vet bill, too!"

"I forgot about that," James said. "I figured Pat donated his charges for fixing up Tucker, but maybe not. Maybe it was someone else."

"But *who*?" Marta pressed. "I should question my dad, but I don't think he has that kind of money after covering all my mother's final expenses. I certainly hope he wouldn't put himself in financial jeopardy for me! I shouldn't have even told Dad about putting the house up for sale. I'm sure it has worried him."

James was accustomed to Marta calling David her dad. He was, after all. He and his wife Alice had adopted Marta when she was only a few days old. James might be her father, but David was her dad.

"I think your dad is wiser than that," he assessed. "He might have helped with the vet bill but probably not the house. Who else could have done that?"

"I don't know!" Marta moaned. "It must have been Pat, don't you think?"

"Well, whoever has done this has a generous heart and will be gratified just knowing they have helped you out," James finally said. "It is up to you to graciously accept the gift and carry on with your life."

"But how do I face Pat again without wondering if he was the one? And if it was not him, then do I have to wonder about every person I meet? I would rather know who to thank!" A heavy sigh slumped her shoulders.

"A person who is that generous does not expect to be thanked," James counseled. "All they would want is for you to be happy."

Marta stood to go. "Oh, I am happy, for sure! And Jannah will be sporting her happy smile again—she seems to have lost it lately."

James nodded in agreement. "Yes, the news will be the perfect cure for Miss Jannah's gloom. Have her come tell me after you tell her, and I will act like I didn't know."

"I'll do that!" Marta agreed, their conspiracy sealed with a smile as she headed for the door.

CHAPTER FOURTEEN

PAT PUSHED AWAY FROM HIS desk and headed to the kennel to check on the boarded animals before leaving for the night. A spirited chorus from dogs and cats greeted him as he came through the door. He stopped at every cage and talked quietly to each animal, taking a few extra minutes to inspect those who were there recuperating from surgeries.

His mind wandered back to the days when Tucker had stayed there. From the moment he saw him and Jannah on the side of the road, Pat was heavily invested. The memory alone ripped his heart open. He knew he had to save the dog's life somehow. Even his hands had shaken before the surgery because the outcome would impact the rest of Jannah's life. In a small way, he had felt a positive outcome could make restitution for the young life he had taken years ago.

He had said a silent prayer before Tucker's surgery, as he did before each surgery he performed. Any animal who was loved enough to be brought for veterinarian care must belong to someone very attached to it. Pat did everything in his power to restore those animals to health.

The incident had knitted Pat's heart to Tucker's family. He had found himself looking forward to the dog's follow-up appointments. At first, Jannah had watched him with fear on her face. But she had gradually relaxed and brought Tucker to the clinic with a smile on her face, confident her best friend was mending. Or perhaps, she was just more confident in Pat.

Pat had to admit he anticipated opportunities to see Jannah's mother. When he realized Marta had lost a son and her husband in such horrible ways, his heart opened to her. Living through the death of a child was an experience that could not be explained in words. Marta would understand his own nightmare of a life ended too soon.

He smiled to himself, remembering the moment when she had learned the bill for Tucker's care had been covered. The relief on her face told Pat right then that Marta was struggling financially. She was so thankful. Pat was thankful, too, for the anonymous person who cared so much for Marta.

Pat also remembered his commitment to deny any feelings he might ever have for a woman. There could be children from those feelings, and he could not deal with the possibility of losing one of them. It could happen. Marta had already lost one child. Even if he did allow his feelings for Marta to grow, was she ready for another relationship? Would she ever be? Would he just be setting himself up for disappointment?

After the last animal was cared for, Pat left the kennel and flipped off the light. His day was over. Time to go home to his quiet, empty house. He wondered what going home to a family would feel like. But he shook his head, chasing away those thoughts. Better to guard his heart than face the despair of losing someone he loved.

As he pulled out of the clinic's parking lot, he paused in indecision. Should he drive by Marta's house? Maybe Tucker would be outside playing. Maybe Jannah would be with him. Maybe Marta would be sitting on the porch. Maybe he could stop and visit a few minutes. He turned down her street, his decision made.

As his car approached their home, he could see Marta at the door, probably calling for Jannah to come inside. Pat could not drive by Marta's house without having to turn around to exit the cul-de-sac. He had to stop now. Marta would see him. She *did* see him. She started waving before he pulled into her driveway. It was a welcoming wave, and Pat tossed aside all the questions that had nettled his thoughts the last few minutes.

Putting the car into park and turning off the engine, he shoved his long legs out the door of the Jeep and looked over his shoulder for Tucker and Jannah. From the yard next door, Tucker barked. Jannah chased after him, her pony tail whipping in the breeze.

"Hey, you two!" Pat bent down on one knee to accommodate the sloppy greeting from Tucker. Panting from the run, Jannah halted only a couple steps behind Tucker and sucked in some deep breaths.

"Tucker, stop licking Dr. Watson!" Jannah scolded between breaths. "You know you aren't supposed to do that!"

Pat ran his hand down the back of the big dog. "Oh, Jannah, it's okay. I get this kind of welcome from only my very best friends!" Tucker wagged his tail and tipped his head up to beg for scratches.

"We've been over at Grandpa Hawkeye's playing Frisbee with him," Jannah explained. "Here, Tucker, show Dr. Watson how you can catch!" She tossed the Frisbee in the air, and the dog bounded after it. When the disc was a few feet above the ground, Tucker leaped up and snagged it with his teeth. His hindquarters flailed awkwardly until his front feet landed him firmly on the ground. Celebrating the catch, Tucker returned and dropped the Frisbee at Jannah's feet.

"Good job, Tucker!" Pat cheered. Tucker bounced back and forth between Jannah and Pat, relishing their words of encouragement like his favorite treats.

Jannah wrapped her arms around the dog's neck and buried her face in his fur. "Can you believe that, Dr. Watson? Did you see how Tucker caught the Frisbee in the air?"

"Yes, I did!" Pat replied. "You have really been working with him, haven't you?" Pat opened his arms to embrace the little girl and her beloved dog. How perfectly they both fit into the lonely spaces in his heart. "Keep practicing, Tucker," Pat urged. "Throw it again, Jannah!" Pat stood and watched the pair disappear around the corner of the house. With the chase now in the backyard, Pat headed to the front door, where Marta waited.

"So, I have some good news to share," Marta whispered to Pat when he got to the door. The secret sparkled in her eyes.

"Really? Spill it!"

"My house loan has been paid off." Marta giggled.

"Whoa!" he grinned. "That really *is* good news! Did your ship come in, or what?"

Marta stepped back and eyed him closely. "*Someone's* ship must have come in," she answered. "The bank would not tell me who paid off the loan. It certainly wasn't me!"

The smile on Pat's face widened. "Marta, if you are asking if I did that for you, I wish I could tell you I did. I didn't, but I could just hug whoever it was!"

Marta leaned over the railing to keep an eye on Jannah and Tucker running back toward James' yard. "Oh, Pat, it is so frustrating not knowing who did this! Who else could have done such a thing?"

Pat stepped up behind her, wrapping his arms around her shoulders. He snuggled close to her hair and breathed in the smell of her. "Do you think your father might have paid off the loan for you?"

Marta shook her head. "No, I don't think it was him. I don't think he has that kind of money."

"Maybe James?"

"He claims not."

Pat turned Marta around to face him. "The bank didn't give any clues? Would they tell you more if you asked?"

"They said the person wished to remain anonymous," Marta said. "That puts me in a very awkward position."

Pat lifted Marta's chin with a finger. "I am certain the mystery person would not want you to feel so frustrated with their gift. Maybe you will learn their identity sometime in the future. For now? Just be happy you don't have to move after all!"

"That is exactly what James told me," Marta confessed. "So, I guess I just stop worrying about 'who done it' and let life get back to normal—whatever that is!"

"That's exactly what you should do! Let's go get rid of the 'For Sale' sign, what do you say?" Pat reached for Marta's hand, pulling her toward the steps.

Perhaps his heart was already too involved with Marta. The news Marta and Jannah would not be moving was a relief, as much for himself as for Marta. The look on Marta's face was one of release from unbearable pressure. Someone certainly loved Marta very much to be willing to pay off her house loan! Could James be the one? He was just a neighbor, wasn't he? What was the real connection between Marta and the man Jannah called "Grandpa Hawkeye"?

CHAPTER FIFTEEN

THE FRONT DOOR OPENED, AND Jannah flew into the kitchen where James was pouring a cup of coffee.

"Grandpa Hawkeye! Guess what?" Jannah's voice crackled with excitement.

James put the coffee cup down and turned to greet the child. "What is it?" he asked, trying to conceal any hint he already knew what she would say.

"You won't believe this!" Jannah began. She was jumping up and down now, her hair bouncing around her face.

"Well, then you *must* tell me what it is!" James prodded.

"We don't have to move!" Jannah cried. "Mommy doesn't have to sell the house!"

James grabbed the child's hands and began to jump around the kitchen with her. He grinned as he absorbed Jannah's delight. He had hoped Marta would not wait too long to tell Jannah because he wasn't sure how long he could keep the secret!

"That is the best news I have had in a long time!"

"I know!" Jannah agreed. "I couldn't wait to tell you!" She squeezed James' hands in her own, her face beaming with pure joy.

"How about a soda to celebrate?" James offered.

"That would be great!"

James pulled a can from his pantry and put ice in a glass. "There are some cookies in the cabinet. Pick which kind you want to open."

Jannah sorted through the options and selected the chocolate and coconut cookies they both liked.

"Bring them out on the deck," James told her. He carried the soda and his coffee cup as they headed out the patio door. James opened the cookies and set them on the table. "Help yourself!"

"Can you believe it?" Jannah shook her head in disbelief while she nibbled on the cookie in her hand.

James smiled at the child. "It is just the best news you could ever tell me! You know something, Jannah? I have been asking God if He couldn't find some way to let you stay in your house so we could always be neighbors, and it looks as if He has done just that!" He leaned in close to her face and whispered, "Besides, I was so dreading having to train another little girl to pull weeds and not flowers!"

"Oh, Grandpa!" Jannah giggled. "I knew you would be sad if I moved."

"Sad?" James' eyebrows arched high. "I would have been heartbroken," he corrected. "There is no one else I would rather have for neighbors than you and your mother!"

"But you would have missed Tucker just a little, too, wouldn't you?" Jannah peered over the brim of her glass at him.

"Oh, yes!" James assured her. "The next little girl's dog would probably have dug holes in all my flower beds!" He looked around, frowning. "Where is Tucker, by the way?"

Jannah whipped her head around as if she expected to find the dog at her side. "I forgot to bring him!" she said with a laugh. "I was so excited when Mommy told me we are not moving, I ran out the door to come tell you, and I forgot to bring Tucker!" She stuffed a cookie in her mouth and slurped soda through her straw. "I will tell him next. He will be very happy, too!"

"No doubt! I can't imagine not having you and Tucker for neighbors. Your visits are extra special to me!"

"We would have found a way to visit you, anyway," Jannah said.

"I should hope so!" James patted Jannah's arm and reached for another cookie. "I would have found a way to come visit you, too! But isn't this much better? Nothing will be changing!"

Jannah swallowed the last of her cookie and finished her soda. "Gotta go tell Tucker," she announced as she hopped out of her chair. At the top step of the deck, she turned to face James again. Her nose was screwed up into thoughtful concentration. "Do you *really* think that God was responsible for us not having to move?"

"Oh, yes, Jannah, I *really* do think God is responsible for this good news! And I intend to spend a few minutes thanking Him!"

James watched Jannah bounce down the deck steps and around the corner of the house. As soon as the child was out of sight, he wiped at the tears crowding the corners of his eyes. He headed for his bedroom and settled down into his wife's rocking chair. It was time to thank God!

CHAPTER SIXTEEN

THE KEY SLID IN THE lock. That would be Elizabeth. Donna had asked her to come. It was time to tell her about the sister she had never known.

"Hey, Mom!" Elizabeth greeted her from the hallway.

"In here, Elizabeth," Donna replied.

"I have a few things to stick in the refrigerator, and then I will be right there."

Donna smoothed the front of her shirt as her heart threatened to beat out of her chest. The discussion would not be easy. She had tried to imagine how Elizabeth would react. Those thoughts alone almost prevented Donna from sharing her secret, but she had locked the existence of the other daughter deep inside her soul for too long. It was time for the truth.

"Want some coffee?" Elizabeth asked from the kitchen.

"Not now," Donna replied, "but help yourself."

Elizabeth entered the room and sat on the couch opposite her mother. "You look good, Mom," she said.

"I am feeling a lot better," Donna said.

Elizabeth looked about the room. "The house looks great! The home health service is doing a good job."

Donna sighed. "Yes, they are. I couldn't manage without their help. Thanks for arranging it for me."

"Thanks for accepting the help," Elizabeth replied. "I know it wasn't what you wanted at first." She took a sip from her steaming cup. "I was planning to come see in you in a couple weeks, but it sounded pretty urgent when you called yesterday."

Donna swallowed the lump in her throat. "Yes, it is urgent," she began. "I have put this off far too long, and it has only become more and more difficult the longer I have waited."

"What are you talking about, Mom?" Elizabeth asked, her voice taut.

"I thought I should tell all three of you children together, but lately, I have decided it might be best to tell you first. You are my only other daughter, after all."

"*Other* daughter?" Elizabeth quizzed. "What do you mean?"

Donna stared down at her hands and sucked in a deep breath. "I had another daughter when I was only seventeen. My parents insisted I place her for adoption."

"*What?*" Elizabeth's coffee cup thunked on the table, and she jumped up, confusion shaking her body. "Why have you never told me this before? Why tell me *now?*"

"Not even your father knows about my first child," Donna whispered. "It has tormented me for many years. I needed to tell you to relieve the burden the secret has been for me." Donna searched her daughter's face, silently pleading for understanding.

Elizabeth walked away from Donna and stared out the window. When she turned back to face her mother, her eyes burned with rage. "How could you give away your own child?"

"My parents gave me no other options. They sent me away from their home until the baby was born." She paused to choke back the tears before they drowned her. "They did not even come to see the baby at the hospital. And I never returned to my parents' home."

The silence pushed them further apart. A sick feeling in Donna's heart billowed up to her throat. She already had one daughter and grandchild who were strangers to her. Had she just alienated Elizabeth and destroyed her chance to be a part of Kendra's life, too? It was time to claim God's promise in Romans 8:28 that all of this would work for good.

Elizabeth finally spoke. "Are your parents dead, as you have always told us? Or is there more you need to tell me about them as well?" Her hands hung in fists at her side. "I just don't understand how a mother can give up her own child!"

"Yes, Elizabeth, my parents passed away. They died in a car wreck when you were very young, like I told you." Donna paused, mustering the courage to continue. "When the baby was born, I had no job, no place to live, and no husband to help me. I held that child one time after she was born for about five minutes. She was perfect. Her little fingers wrapped around mine. Her dark hair was silky soft. Her skin felt like peach fuzz. They took her from my arms and told me I would not be able to hold her again. I cried for hours after that. My belly ached, and my arms were empty. But I knew I had made the right decision."

"I don't understand how giving away your own child could ever be a 'right decision'!" Elizabeth hissed the angry words like venom. "And where was the father? Did he refuse to claim the child?"

Donna's shoulders slumped, and her head hung low. "My parents refused any contact between me and the baby's father after I told them I was pregnant. I found out years later, he tried multiple times to contact me. He did come to the hospital the day she was born because I called him myself, but it was too late for him to hold her. He could only look at her through the nursery window." Sobs broke Donna's voice. "He said we could have made it work somehow, if only he had been able to talk to me. But it was too late."

"So, do you know where this *child* is now? Have you kept that from us as well?" Elizabeth stood across the room from her mother, her arms crossed.

Here was the hard part—the admission Donna had continued the charade. "The child's father has been in touch with me for the last couple years. He located our daughter and now lives in the same city where she lives."

Elizabeth's mouth dropped open, and she shook her head in disbelief. "And does she know he is there?"

"She does now. He didn't tell her at first, and it almost ruined everything when she found out he had not explained himself from the beginning."

"And does she know who her biological mother is and where you live?" Elizabeth fired the questions at Donna faster than she could think.

"Her father has told her about me," Donna admitted. "But she has not asked to meet me, and I have not asked to meet her."

"Why *haven't* you?" Elizabeth exploded.

"Because I want a meeting to be *her* choice," Donna replied in a whisper.

"I suppose it would be difficult for you to explain why all of a sudden you wanted to be a part of her life after you gave her away as a baby." A frosty tone chilled Elizabeth's words.

Donna had no response to the accusation. It was true. How *would* she explain why she wanted to see her daughter now?

"Does this other daughter have a name?"

"Her name is Marta Newton. And she has a daughter named Jannah."

"So, Kendra is *not* your only grandchild!" Elizabeth turned back to the window.

"No," Donna replied. "Jannah is about the same age as Kendra."

"Isn't that nice?" Elizabeth spat out. "Maybe they can be best friends one day!"

Donna bent her head, disheartened by Elizabeth's fierce anger. "I doubt that would ever happen," she replied. "I have not even met Jannah."

"Oh, I am sure you will eventually. And you will want us all to be one big, happy family."

"No, Elizabeth," Donna objected. "I would never ask that of any of you. But if the opportunity ever comes for me to meet them, I will not pass it up." She looked directly into her daughter's eyes. "You need to understand that."

CHAPTER SEVENTEEN

MARTA STILL WRESTLED WITH QUESTIONS about the mysterious payment of her house loan. She found herself preoccupied, watching for looks or listening for clues whenever she was with James or Pat. Her dad had expressed genuine surprise when she told them the news, and it confirmed her suspicions that it wasn't he who helped her.

She also found herself looking forward to Pat's visits or phone calls. Nothing about him was pushy, and she appreciated that even more than his good looks and his easy way with Jannah. The child's face beamed a happy smile when Pat was around. He never turned down an opportunity to play with Tucker.

Pat had asked her out for dinner a few nights ago. Actually, he asked both Marta and Jannah to join him, but Jannah had a classmate's birthday party to attend the same evening. It wasn't a dress-up date— just a chance to munch a sandwich and chat across the table from each other. But it had felt like a date to Marta. She had spent more time than usual picking out the clothes to wear and touching up her make-up before Pat arrived. More than that, when Pat had kissed her on the cheek before leaving, tingles of delight had raced up her back and warmed her neck.

It had been a long time since she had been kissed. She wasn't sure how she felt about the attraction growing between the two of them. She wasn't afraid it was too soon after her husband's death. It had been over two years. And she couldn't imagine that Jannah would disapprove.

Her uncertainty made no sense to her. She needed to talk it out with someone, and James was the perfect person.

Marta slipped on her shoes and headed out the door. "I'm going over to visit with Grandpa Hawkeye for a few minutes," she shouted to Jannah in the backyard.

"Okay, Mom!" Jannah replied.

Marta hoped Tucker would distract Jannah, so she could visit with James alone. She sighed with relief when she heard Jannah encouraging the dog to fetch. The two were in serious training mode, and she would not be followed.

"Anyone home?" she asked through the open front door.

"I'm on the deck," James shouted. "Come on through and join me!"

Marta kicked off her flip flops inside the door and carried them through the house. James' house was as impeccable as his flower gardens. The morning newspaper was folded in half and placed on the stand next to his recliner. The aroma of freshly-brewed coffee warmed the air. There were no dishes to be seen anywhere, not even in the drainer. *Amazing*, Marta thought. She pushed the patio screen door to the side and found James reclined in a lawn chair with an opened book on his lap.

"It is hot enough to be the first day of school!" Marta exclaimed as she pushed her toes back into her shoes.

"That's right around the corner, isn't it?"

"Two weeks away, but who's counting?" Marta pulled up an empty deck chair and settled down opposite James. "I'm actually looking forward to getting back into the routine," she admitted.

"It has been a busy summer for you, hasn't it?"

Marta sighed and nodded in wonder. "Oh yeah! A lot has happened since Tucker's accident."

"Things have turned out well, though." His positivity was one of the qualities Marta appreciated about him the most.

"Definitely," Marta agreed. "Better than I hoped."

"Still wondering who paid off the house loan?" James guessed.

"That is part of what is keeping my brain in turmoil." Marta chuckled. She pushed stray hairs behind her ear and swallowed hard.

"What else is going on?" James pressed.

Marta's lips twisted in thought before she answered. "I need to talk to you about Pat."

James put his book aside and put his feet on the deck, facing Marta. "Okay. Let's talk."

"Do you like him?" She cocked her head and squinted her eyes, waiting for James' response.

"I do," James said softly. "Do you?"

"Yes, I do." Marta nodded.

"Does Jannah like him?"

"Oh, yes, she thinks he is the most wonderful man alive—well, maybe second only to Grandpa Hawkeye!" Marta reached over and shoved James' knee. "You know," she continued, "*you* can do nothing wrong as far as Jannah is concerned!"

"You like Pat, and Jannah likes Pat, and I like Pat. So, what's the problem?" James smiled and spread his hands wide in summary.

Marta allowed a heavy sigh before answering. "I just don't know if I want to get into another relationship."

"Is Pat being pushy?" Marta sensed her protective father was prepared to pounce.

"Not at all," Marta assured him. "In fact, he might laugh if he knew I was even thinking about a relationship with him."

James scratched his head, pursing his lips. "Oh, I don't think he would laugh. I think he is very interested in you."

"Really?" Marta scooted to the edge of her chair. "What makes you think so?"

"Oh, I don't know. Maybe the fact his Jeep is in your driveway pretty often? Or maybe the fact he always has a smile on his face when he is around you?"

"You have noticed that?" Marta wrinkled her nose like a kid caught in mischief.

"Jannah keeps me pretty informed," James disclosed with a grin. Marta giggled as she watched the ornery smile dance across his lips and wrinkle the corners of his eyes. Indeed, she could imagine her daughter reporting to Grandpa each house visit the veterinarian made to check on Tucker's progress.

"So, you think it would be okay for me to date Pat?"

James leaned to prop his elbows on his knees. "I think Pat has proven himself to be a good friend to you. Whether your relationship goes beyond friendship is a decision you will have to make for yourself."

"I called my dad, but it's hard for him to advise me when he's never met Pat." Marta sighed. "I wish my mother was still alive and could give me her thoughts."

"A mother's opinion becomes more valued the older you get. You had a very good mother." James tipped his head, looking at Marta over his glasses.

"She was the best!" She turned to look out over the deck railing into the shaded yard. The flowers waved at her in the gentle breeze. Her mind wandered to another world she had lately contemplated. "I sometimes wonder what my biological mother is like." She glanced back at James, and he dropped his head. "Do you think I will ever get to meet her?"

"I didn't know if you wanted to meet her," James responded. "I think she would like to meet you and would be pleased to find out you had a happy childhood and good parents."

Marta raised a knee and clasped her hands around it. She rocked back and looked up into the sky. "I cannot imagine giving away my child," Marta mused.

"It was not easy for your biological mother either," James hurried to defend Donna. "She has had a lot of years to wonder what happened to you." He swallowed hard. "Just like I did."

"Do you stay in contact with her?" Marta asked.

"Yes, I do," James admitted. "She had a stroke a few months ago and spent some time in a nursing facility, but she is home now and is getting along well by herself."

"She is by herself? Is she not married?" Marta's curiosity was firing.

"She is divorced. Her husband left her for a much younger woman several years ago," James answered. "She has three children, but none of them lives very close. Her only daughter—besides you—did come to stay with her while she was recovering."

"Do you *really* think she would like to meet me?" Marta leaned toward James, her heart pounding.

"I am certain of it!"

"What is she like?" Marta quizzed. "Do I look like her?"

James laughed quietly. "Oh, yes, you do look like her. I don't have any pictures of her, but I have given her pictures of you and Jannah." James looked away from Marta, a knot forming in his throat. "I didn't ask your permission to do that, but I have felt so guilty getting to know you when your biological mother has not had the same opportunity. I wanted her to at least see what a beautiful woman you have become."

Marta shifted in her chair. This was all beginning to sound familiar. Her biological mother knew what she looked like and where she lived, and she knew about Jannah; but Marta knew almost nothing about her. Things had happened the same way with James. He had found Marta and learned much about her before disclosing his identity to her. "Have you met her other children?" Marta's voice was soft, the excitement tamed by her disconcerting comparisons.

"I ran into her daughter once when I was visiting her mother after the stroke. The boys I have met only in pictures, as well as her only grandchild," James raised his eyes back to Marta's face.

"Do they know about me?" The information about this family gathered in her mind like puzzle pieces. Soon, she would have to decide if it was a puzzle she wanted to complete.

"I do not know," James admitted. "Would you like me to ask?"

"I'm not sure." Marta rubbed her hands down the front of her shorts. "I came here questioning a relationship with a man, and now I am contemplating a new relationship with my biological mother. I just don't know if I am emotionally up to all this."

"It is a lot to think about." James nodded. "I have not encouraged a meeting between you and your biological mother because I did not want it to be something you agreed to for my sake. It needs to be something you decide to do for your own reasons."

Marta stood, moving to the deck steps where she could see Jannah still playing with Tucker in their backyard. "I don't know, James. I don't know if I want to open that can of worms. How would I explain it all to Jannah?"

"I understand. You have had a lot to deal with the last couple years. Take your time making your decisions. Regrets are not easy to live with."

"Do you have many regrets, James?" Marta asked quietly. She turned back to him, terrified of finding the truth in his eyes. "Am I one of them?"

James shook his head. "No! Teenagers do a lot of things without thinking through the consequences. They can't even comprehend the consequences sometimes. It was a bad decision to be sexually involved with someone before I was married. I understand now that God has a better plan for every man and every woman, but I didn't understand that at the time. A child was conceived. A baby was born and given to a family who wanted her very much and loved her very much. I cannot regret that the baby was born when she has grown into such a beautiful young woman who has provided joy to all who know her." James halted and lifted his face to Marta. "My only regret is I was not the man who was privileged to raise her. I will always be grateful to your father for doing such a fine job in my place!"

Marta returned to James' side, kneeling in front of him with tears in her eyes. "James, thank you. Thank you for saying such a thing." Emotions almost choked out her words. "I'm so glad you searched for me and allowed me to get to know you. You've always honored my parents, and you are such a good grandpa to Jannah. Thank you." She blinked, and a few of her tears escaped.

James' own face was streaked with tears. "I love you, Marta," he whispered. "I thank God every day for the opportunity He has given me to know you. It has been an undeserved blessing."

"You are a good man, James," Marta replied. "I have come to love you very much, too. And Jannah would fight for you! You know that, don't you?"

James chuckled as he swiped at his tears. "Yes, I guess I do."

CHAPTER EIGHTEEN

ELIZABETH SAT AT HER DESK, reading through the letter she had written to her mother. Her anger toward her mother had continued to boil for days. Why did her mother keep Marta's existence a secret all these years? Why share the news now? Elizabeth walked out of her mother's house that day with intentions of never returning. Her mother could look to her *first* daughter for any assistance she needed in the future!

She was tortured by her racing thoughts. Writing a letter seemed like the only way to relieve those thoughts. Whether she ever sent the letter to her mother or not. And would she? Should she? She turned back to the paper she held in her hands. A knot had formed in her stomach while she wrote the letter, and it tightened as she reread the words.

Dear Mother,

I cannot begin to explain to you the feelings I have had since you told me about the daughter you gave away. Nor can I understand how a mother could turn her back on a newborn that way. As you know, I had much difficulty getting pregnant with Kendra. It is inconceivable I would ever have so little regard for a life I had created, I would toss it out to be rescued by strangers!

Yes, you did toss "it" out! You took the easy way out and abandoned a baby so you would not have to deal with the consequences of getting pregnant. The only worse thing you could have done would have been to have an abortion. I don't even want to know if you considered that option.

And what about the father? You told me your parents would not allow you any contact with him. Really? You obviously did other things your parents didn't want you to do. Was there no way the two of you could have figured out a way to raise the child together? I doubt the father was anyone worth having around, anyway, since he let you bear all the burden of the pregnancy!

It is clear you have been thinking about reconnecting with this child. I hope you think about it a long time before you take any action. Think about the consequences of introducing this person to our already fragmented family. Think about how your other children might feel. And what about your granddaughter? The one you have met, I mean. Suddenly there is another granddaughter who is the center of your attention.

I wonder now if my father had found out about this lie you were living? Is that why he left us? Did he feel betrayed by a wife who had kept this secret from him for so many years? I have condemned him for the choices he made, but perhaps now I can understand what drove him to another woman!

It is going to take me some time to answer all these questions. While I am struggling to work through all this, I hope you will also think about the effects of your choices—choices you made years ago, as well as the choices you have ahead of you.

Love,

Elizabeth

Elizabeth folded the paper and placed it in an envelope. She wiped at the tears slipping down her cheeks. There was so much anger in those words, but there was undeniable consolation from letting the words out of her heart. She tucked the envelope into the desk drawer. She needed more time to decide if she would send it.

CHAPTER NINETEEN

JAMES PICKED UP HIS CELL phone, eager to make the call. He'd waited a long time for this, and now he had permission. He hoped his voice wouldn't tremble like his hands were. The line rang several times.

Just when he thought the call would go to voicemail, Donna's faint voice replied, "Hello?"

"Donna? This is James. Is everything okay?" A nasty fear crept up James' neck. Her voice did not sound right.

"Oh, hello, James." Donna cleared her throat before continuing. "I guess I fell asleep. I'm sorry it took so long for me to answer."

"Sorry I woke you." James' shoulders relaxed in relief. "Would you like me to call back later?"

"Goodness, no!" Donna insisted. "I can sleep any time. I would much rather visit with you!"

"Great! I think I have some good news for you." James grinned in childish pleasure, his heart bursting to fulfill the one wish Donna had suppressed for so many years.

"Really? Don't keep me in suspense!"

"How would you feel about meeting Marta?" James held his breath waiting for Donna's reaction. There was only silence, and James feared he had suggested something Donna had decided against. "Donna? Did you hear me?"

"Yes, James, I heard you." Donna's voice quivered. "I just don't know what to say. Meeting Marta is something I have dreamed of for a very long time. I wonder if I am dreaming now."

"You're not dreaming, Donna. Marta asked me to find out if she could come with me the next time I come to visit you. So, what do you think?" James grinned again, imagining the hope spreading across Donna's face.

"Was it her idea?" Donna's voice dropped, concern lacing her tone. "This isn't something you asked her to do, is it?"

"No. We talked about you, and Marta made the request without any coaching on my part."

Donna's voice filled with tears. "I would very much like to meet her, James! When can you make the trip?"

"School starts in a week, and Marta is pretty busy preparing for that. She wondered if it would work for us to come the end of September?"

"Definitely!" Then a heavy sigh sounded on Donna's end. "What if she is disappointed in how she finds me?"

"Disappointed? Why would Marta be disappointed?" There was no chance Marta would come with unrealistic expectations.

"I am an old woman, living alone in a big old house, dependent upon a walker and unable to do much of anything for myself."

James swallowed a lump in his throat. It had not been so long ago when he met Marta for the first time, and he well remembered the trepidation that nearly cost him the opportunity to meet his only child. "Marta is a very gracious lady, Donna," he replied tenderly. "She has had her share of difficulties, and she will understand your situation. I am certain she will overlook so many of those things. It took her several days to make this decision. She is not doing this on a whim. Nor is she doing it at my encouragement. She simply wants to meet you."

"And I want to meet her!" A new confidence brightened Donna's voice. "Please tell her I am looking forward to seeing her!"

"Shall we plan on the last Saturday in September, then?"

"That sounds good to me. And, James?"

"Yes?"

"Will Jannah be coming, too?"

"Not this time, Donna," James replied. "This time, it will be just Marta and me."

"All right," Donna said, but the disappointment in her voice was impossible to miss.

James ached to assure Donna there would be other opportunities to become acquainted with both Marta and Jannah. But he would not offer a promise he might not be able to fulfill. For now, meeting Marta would have to be enough.

CHAPTER TWENTY

MARTA LEANED ON THE KITCHEN counter and watched Pat climb out of his vehicle. Jannah and Tucker were playing in the front yard, and she knew Pat would stop to chat with them before coming to the house. She enjoyed every opportunity to watch the man interact with her daughter.

The two of them had connected in a special way during Tucker's recuperation. Jannah was convinced Dr. Pat had saved her dog's life, and she owed him her devotion for the rest of her life! Marta smiled when Pat knelt and rubbed Tucker's neck. Judging by the wagging tail, there was little doubt that Tucker had grown just as fond of Dr. Pat as Jannah had.

When Pat stood and started toward the house, Marta moved away from the window and reached to smooth her hair back from her face. She had to admit a visit from Pat perked up her spirits, and she found herself glancing in the mirror when she knew he was on the premises.

"Knock, knock!" Pat yelled through the screened door.

"Hey, Pat!" Marta greeted in return. "Come on in!"

Pat pulled her close and wrapped his arms around her shoulders. "Good to see you," he whispered, nuzzling against her hair.

"Likewise," Marta replied with a contented sigh. She glanced out the window to see where Jannah was playing. She almost felt guilty when Pat held her this way because she wasn't sure how Jannah would feel about her mother being attracted to another man.

Pat turned to follow her glance. "They are playing," he assured her. "We have a few minutes for this." He grinned and pulled her close again.

Marta relaxed in his arms. "I need to talk to you while Jannah is outside, though," she finally said, pulling free from him and turning to lead him to the front room.

"What's up? Nothing serious, I hope!"

"I need your advice about something, but I have to share some backstory with you before you can understand my situation." Marta motioned for him to sit on the couch as she poured him a cup of iced lemonade.

"This is sounding kind of serious." He wrapped his fingers around the cool glass and looked at Marta with questioning eyes.

Marta settled down on the chair opposite him, sighing heavily. "I probably should have told you this before, but there was no good reason until now." She paused only a moment, hurrying through the information while they were still alone. "I was adopted as a baby. Jannah knows the whole story." She swallowed before revealing the most shocking part. "James is my biological father."

Disbelief washed across Pat's face. "You're kidding, right?"

"No, I am not kidding. I am the only child James ever had. After his wife passed away, he determined to find me. And he did."

"Wow!" Pat whispered. "I guess that explains the relationship he has with Jannah. And you."

"Well, things are good now," Marta nodded, "but there was a time when I was very angry with him for not being up front with me about his identity. As it turned out, he had a good reason for not sharing that with me, but it took me a while to accept his reasons."

"You mean, he pretended to be someone that he wasn't?"

Marta hurried to defend James' secrecy. "Well, he didn't really 'pretend,' but he didn't tell me he was my father until after he moved into our neighborhood."

"So, how did you find out?" Pat pressed.

Marta turned to look out the window to check on Jannah and Tucker. Satisfied they were still entertained outside, she sighed. "It started when

I was in the hospital with a gunshot wound. James offered to donate blood for me, but when they typed his blood, it was not compatible with mine. It should have been if he was truly my biological father."

"Whoa! Hold on! You had a gunshot wound? What happened?" Concern flooded Pat's face.

Marta's lips curled to one side. "It's another long story. The short version is that I was accidentally hit with a bullet, and I lost a lot of blood. I will tell you more about it another time."

"So, is James your father, or isn't he?"

"At that point, James began to question that himself. To make matters worse, my biological mother told him she was not certain he was my father, and it might have been another man. That devastated James! For all these years, he had believed he had a daughter somewhere. The blood test convinced him he had been wrong to search for me." Another deep sigh escaped Marta's lips. "He finally decided to confront my mother face-to-face, and she admitted she lied to him about there being another man. But James wanted to be certain—and that's why he had to tell me. We had to do a paternity test."

"He just came right out and asked you to do the test?"

Marta looked away from him. "Well, not exactly. I suggested it. When he told me he was my father—or thought he was my father—I became very angry and told him to stay away from me and Jannah. He got in his car and drove away. I took a lot of time to think about how I had reacted, and I realized James had been only very kind and helpful to me through everything that happened with my husband. And I could not ignore how much Jannah loved him."

Marta's shoulders heaved with the weight of all the memories. "I waited and waited for James to return so I could apologize. I did not see him come home the first night, and I was so worried about him. But to my relief, he was home the next morning. He went jogging as always, so I followed him after he passed our house. When I finally got him to stop, I told him how sorry I was for the things I had said.

That's when I suggested we do whatever needed to be done to find out if he really is my father."

"So, what did you have to do? How did you find out?"

"It was a simple swab test," Marta answered. "We went to the hospital lab, and the inside of our cheeks were swabbed. I remember thinking it surely had to take something more complicated than that to determine parentage! But that's all there was to it—plus a very long, twenty-four hour wait for the results."

"Wow! I had no idea what a paternity test involved!" Pat shook his head in disbelief.

"Me neither!" Marta responded. "James called the lab at the end of the next day, and he was told it was a positive match!"

Pat leaned forward, gathering Marta's hand into his. He squeezed her fingers and cocked his head. "How did you feel when you found out?"

"I already knew I was adopted, so I didn't have to deal with that part of it," Marta began. "And James was a very dear friend by that time. So, I just felt relief that James finally had the confirmation he had wanted for so many years."

"What has James told you about your biological mother?" Pat scooted to the edge of his chair.

"Only bits and pieces. She lives about five hours away. She's divorced. Her ex-husband is a doctor. She has other children and one granddaughter. She recently suffered a stroke, but she is recovering well from that . . ." Marta raised her shoulders, looking into Pat's eyes. "She wants to meet me. That's why I need your advice."

"From me?" Pat pushed back and tapped his chest. "I don't really know what to say. I am sure you have weighed the pros and cons of being introduced. What do you think?"

Marta stood and stepped up to the window to check on Jannah. "I guess I have tried to put myself in my mother's position, and I can only imagine what a hole there must be in her heart having given birth to a child she doesn't even know. I think that would be awful!"

Pat held out his hand as Marta returned to her seat and pulled her down beside him on the couch. He wrapped his arm around her shoulders, snuggling her close. "You are a very wise woman, Marta," he said. "I know you have been considering this opportunity carefully and have been thinking how it would affect both you and Jannah."

"Wise?" Marta questioned. "I don't know about that. I don't want to cause Jannah any unnecessary confusion or unhappiness, but I am curious about my biological mother. James told my mother it would be just him and me coming this time—not Jannah. So, if she turns out to be less than I hope for, I would not have to involve Jannah."

Pat tugged her closer, resting his chin on her head. "Marta, you are such a good mother. I think you have made the right decision—to meet your mother first and then decide whether or not to share Jannah with her. Have you decided when to make the trip? I could have Jannah spend that day with me at the clinic and help care for the boarded pets."

Marta smiled up at him. "What to do with Jannah when I go is part of the problem. James asked my mother about the last weekend in September. School will have started, and my classroom will be in order. It would probably be an overnight trip, since she lives five hours from here. Would you be willing to keep Jannah overnight?"

"Of course!" Pat grinned. "Tucker could come and stay, too. I'm sure that's the only way Jannah would agree to it!"

"Oh, I don't know." Marta laughed. "Jannah is pretty fond of you, and she would jump at the chance to help at the clinic!"

"It's a deal then!" Pat clapped his knees. "Just let me know the date, and I will put it on my calendar."

CHAPTER TWENTY-ONE

DONNA DROPPED THE LETTER INTO her lap and reached for a tissue to wipe her eyes. It had been a mistake to keep Marta a secret from Elizabeth, and this letter proved it. Elizabeth was angry, and Donna could not blame her.

Elizabeth asked many questions Donna could not answer. It was impossible to climb back into the brain of that seventeen-year-old girl who had found herself pregnant and ostracized by her family. It was so long ago, even though the pain was still raw.

She had not told Elizabeth the part about being disowned by her parents. She had never come to terms with that herself. Even though she had placed Marta for adoption at birth, she could not imagine how parents could throw out a child whom they had nurtured for seventeen years—especially when that child needed support more than ever! Teenage pregnancies happened all the time now, but it was a rare thing all those years ago. Still, how could her parents be so cruel?

How could Donna describe to Elizabeth the shame and fear she felt as the pregnancy progressed? It was hidden for a time; but eventually, the word had spread, and Donna and her baby were whispered about in every circle—at school, at church, at her father's job. There was no mistaking the embarrassment and disappointment she had been to her parents. She had seen it in their eyes as they watched her belly grow. She had heard it in their words when they announced she would have to go live at a home for unwed mothers. It had echoed in her heart when there was no communication from them upon the birth of their grandchild. It had been as if Donna had never existed.

Had abortion really been an option for Donna, as Elizabeth had suggested? Not for a small-town girl with no money—unless the abortion was self-inflicted. There was no internet for research on methods, only hushed conversation at the mother's home from girls who had considered it but knew more than Donna about the consequences of a botched attempt.

Fortunately, the mother's home was a ministry of a church and offered spiritual counseling. The girls who decided to keep their babies were connected to employers who had job openings. They were provided names of groups or individuals who were willing to offer day care. Available housing options were listed out for them. Every attempt to keep the mother and child together was made.

For those who chose to place their babies for adoption, the home connected the babies with couples who had been pre-approved. Backgrounds and financial situations were reviewed. The girls were not allowed to know the names or addresses of the couples, only that the home had vetted them. The adoption decision was final when the young mother signed over her rights. For those girls, only a few minutes were allowed with the baby at delivery.

Donna had been one of those young mothers. In her head, she knew there were plenty of couples out there who were unable to have children; in her heart, she hoped her baby would end up with wonderful parents. After delivery, she stood at the nursery window, wondering what life with her baby would have been like. Then she returned to her hospital room to cry in guttural agony. The crying and guilt continued for days, weeks, months. Donna had wondered if the tears would ever stop.

Each year on Marta's birthday, Donna would open the envelope where she kept the baby's tiny footprints. The handwritten date and location of the birth grew faint as the years passed, but the inky footprints remained. Each year, Donna traced the shape of the tiny feet with her fingertip, imagining how big the feet would have grown. There were no pictures, no locks of hair, no crocheted booties to fuel her memories. Only one set of tiny footprints to prove the existence of a life Donna had given away.

Her joy at the births of her subsequent children was always somewhat diminished by the residual guilt from giving away her first. How could she be a good mother if she had done something so despicable? If her husband ever found out about that first child, would he leave her and take the other children with him? She always feared becoming too emotionally attached to her babies, only to be separated if her dark secret was ever revealed. Though she loved them, she dared not hold them too closely.

Now, Elizabeth was walking away from her. What a mess she had made of things! The secret had woven a thread of sorrow through her entire life. Would Elizabeth share the news with her brothers and turn them against their mother, so that her old fear of losing them all would be realized? Donna folded the letter and reached for her Bible. She tucked the paper inside the leather cover, then closed the book and clasped it to her heart. It was time to share her heartache with the One Who loved her in spite of all she had done. It was time to pray for the peace only He could provide.

The words of prayer did not come, not even in a whisper. Only tears. Donna's chest heaved with sobs. She trusted God would see her tears and understand the burden of her heart. She cried until exhaustion stopped her. The Bible slipped to her lap, and her mind shut down in rest. She could only wait for the peace He promised.

Elizabeth stood at the edge of the dining room, watching her daughter's slender fingers dance across the keys of the piano. The girl's long, brown hair was pulled back into a French braid and bound at the bottom with a black stretch tie. She wore teal—a color that accentuated her ivory skin. Kendra was concentrating, completely oblivious of her mother's presence. The recital was in one week, and Kendra determined to have her selection memorized to perfection. She lifted her hands from the keyboard and then relocated her fingers at the bars that needed more practice. Again and again, she played through the difficult measures until the music rang pure.

She was not a disgruntled student who played only to satisfy a pushy parent. Kendra spent hours at the piano, her escape from the silence of her home. Her house knew only the sounds of a single child, and the parents had grown apart from each other. Laughter was rare, so pleasure was sought where it could be found. For Kendra, it was in the connection between her heart and the keys of the piano.

The recital piece was advanced for Kendra's age. Her instructor offered challenging books to keep Kendra pressing forward in her practice. Still, the music seemed to flow naturally from the girl's fingertips, and mastering each piece was simply a matter of turning the pages.

Elizabeth closed her eyes, soaking in the sound of the music. She smiled as she remembered the early years when the sound was anything but soothing. The tentative, out-of-time striking of keys had strung melodies together haphazardly. There were many days of off-key chords, slurred fogginess of an overused sustaining pedal, and sharp shrieks where a flat key should have sounded. Recitals at that stage were painful for students and parents alike!

But now, only delightful sounds filled the house. They prompted Elizabeth to tap her foot in time. To know Kendra found so much comfort in the music also comforted Elizabeth. She had to admit her daughter's accomplishment was a source of pride. No one would miss the astounding difference between the pianists at the recital. Kendra was at the top of her class!

Would her mother also enjoy hearing Kendra play? Her mother! The discord between Elizabeth and her mother crept into nearly every thought. Her mother was incapable of driving for most of the years Kendra took piano lessons, so she had never attended a recital. Elizabeth had shared photos and recital programs with her mother, but her mother's ears had never heard the sweet music.

Her mother would have received the letter by now. At times, Elizabeth wished she had never sent it. But the regrets were quickly drowned by certainty that her feelings were justified.

Elizabeth had not decided to share the news with her brothers yet. Jack would likely have no reaction. He was stationed on the East Coast, a naval officer near retirement. His world was so removed from Elizabeth's, it seemed they could not possibly be from the same family. He had no children—at least, no children that she knew about. Elizabeth got the feeling Jack lived a rather loose life. He was certainly handsome in his military uniform, and he had plenty of money. There had to be women in the picture somewhere.

As for Andrew, no one ever knew where he was. He owned a fleet of semis and drove one himself, crisscrossing the county from one ocean to the other. It was always Andrew, though, who sent flowers to his mother on special occasions. He called regularly to chat with her. And he stopped in to see her when his route allowed. Of course, it had been Andrew who was in trouble at school regularly as well. How many times had Elizabeth overheard the heated conversations between her father and Andrew after the school office called? Unfortunately, those conversations never ended with discipline, and Andrew went right back to his mischief.

Andrew had never married either. Maybe he sensed life on the road would not be good for a marriage. Maybe he lived through his parents' divorce and decided marriage wasn't for him. Maybe he had just never found a girl who could laugh at his ornery nature the way he did. Whatever the reason, he was a loner and seemed happy enough that way.

A tear slipped down Elizabeth's cheek, and she lifted a finger to wipe it away. She looked up to find Kendra watching her.

"Everything okay, Mom?" Kendra tipped her head with narrowing eyes.

Elizabeth forced a smile. "Everything's fine," she assured the girl. "I was just wishing your grandmother could hear you play."

Kendra scooted to the end of the piano bench and propped herself on stiff arms. "We could go see her and take my keyboard!"

"We could, couldn't we?" Elizabeth agreed with feigned enthusiasm. "We will do that sometime." But when? she wondered. She was not ready to face her mother.

CHAPTER TWENTY-TWO

MARTA GLANCED IN THE MIRROR one last time and tucked a stray strand of hair behind her ear. Turning sideways, she pressed her hand down the light sweater resting at her hips. She rubbed her lips together, smoothing her lipstick, and checked her watch for the hundredth time. What if her mother didn't like her? What if she didn't like her mother? What if she did or said something to embarrass James? Meeting her biological mother would put a face to the mental image Marta had construed in her head over the years. What if it was all a let-down?

It turned out to be a good weekend for the trip. The craziness of the first few days of school was behind her, and she was getting comfortable with all the new kids in her class. She had planned the next week's lessons and stayed up later than usual the night before getting all the laundry washed and put away. Thankfully, Jannah was delighted to stay overnight with Dr. Pat and help him tend the boarded animals on Saturday.

Explaining to Jannah why she was taking an overnight trip with Grandpa Hawkeye was uncomfortable. Lying to Jannah was not an option, so Marta simply told Jannah they were making a long trip to meet someone. She suspected Jannah would figure out the mysterious someone was Marta's biological mother, but Jannah accepted the plan without asking questions.

Satisfied she had packed more than she would ever need for the trip, Marta zipped the luggage closed and draped the garment bag over her arm. Her phone jingled in her pocket as she neared the front door. Marta glanced out to make sure James wasn't already waiting before she pulled the phone from her pocket. A smile tugged at her cheeks when she saw Pat's name on the display.

"Hi, Pat!"

"Hey there! Did I catch you before you leave?" Pat sucked in a deep breath.

"You did! What are you doing? You sound winded."

"Oh, we're still doing the boarding chores, but I wanted to tell you goodbye before you left and wish you a good day." Marta heard a cage door rattle and could picture Pat multitasking with his phone squeezed between his shoulder and his ear.

"Get back in there, you ornery pup!" Pat scolded.

"You have an escapee?" she giggled.

"They all think it's time to come out and play since Jannah is here," Pat answered, "but it's not! It is time for breakfast!" There was more rattling of cage doors in the background. Marta could hear Jannah talking to the animals.

"Jannah insisted she be there for feeding time," Marta said. "I know that was earlier than we agreed on."

"Hey! I'm glad to have her help! I'm not sure why, but this is a busy weekend here. We have about two dozen animals boarded."

"Well, that should keep you both busy!" Marta said.

"For sure!" Pat responded. "I hope everything goes well on your trip." There was a pause. "I will miss you," he whispered.

A car pulled into Marta's driveway. "James is here now," she said. "Thanks so much for keeping Jannah occupied." She swallowed a lump before she continued. "I will miss you, too, Pat."

"Get going!" Pat ordered. "See you when you get back!"

James parked in Donna's driveway. He looked over at Marta and saw the hesitancy on her face. "You okay?" he asked quietly.

"I think so," Marta replied. She looked away from him and breathed a heavy sigh.

James reached to pat her leg. "If you have decided not to go through with this, I can go tell Donna, and we will just leave. You know I would do that for you, don't you?" His hand patted her leg again, prodding Marta to look at him.

They had talked late into the night about this encounter. After they had checked into their motel and carried their bags to their rooms, they had headed for the little restaurant the motel clerk had suggested. They had lingered over their burgers until the place was empty of all the other diners. James had covered their tab, and they had driven to a city park he had discovered on one of his earlier trips to see Donna.

Marta had shared a lot with him there under the night sky. She had talked about the accident that had taken her son and about the day Phil had killed himself—and nearly killed her as well. She had talked about the loneliness she had felt afterward and how worried she had been Jannah would never recover emotionally. She had talked about her adoptive parents and how they had helped her survive those tragedies. She had recalled the day James had told her he was her biological father.

James had listened with a heavy heart. His daughter had endured so much. She had assured him his support had been invaluable. How many times had James bowed his head and asked God to give him the words to say to Marta? How many times had James thanked God for allowing him to find her? He had watched the young woman bite her lip and had known she was struggling with another piece of her life's puzzle. He had inwardly prayed God would give her peace.

Now, in the present, Marta laid her hand atop his. "Let's go—before I chicken out," she whispered as she reached for the door handle.

"It will be okay," he assured her. "Donna has wanted to meet you for a very long time. You are making a dream come true for her." He hopped out and walked in stride with Marta as they neared the front door. He knew Donna would be watching and wrestling with her emotions, just as Marta was. He felt God's peace and was eager to witness the reunion.

The door opened before his hand touched the knob. Donna stood at the door with tears rushing down her cheeks. She held the door open with one hand, steadying herself with her other hand on the walker. She pushed it aside to allow a long-imagined embrace. James pulled the door open, standing back to let Marta greet the mother she had never known.

Marta stepped through the door and fell into her mother's arms as naturally as if they had parted only days before. Wrapped in the security of Marta's embrace, Donna turned the walker loose and pulled her daughter close. There were no words—only such raw joy that James was forced to look away. Their tears mingled as they clung to each other. The moment swelled with the passion that had been denied for so many years.

"I am so sorry," Donna whispered through her tears. "I am so very sorry!" Donna's hands patted her daughter's back as if she were comforting a fussing baby.

Marta's silence tugged at James' heart. Was she already regretting this? Finally, he heard his daughter's soft reply. "You made the right decision. We're all going to be okay now." Marta stepped back from Donna and held her by the shoulders. "It's going to be okay."

Donna bowed her head, and her tears fell unchecked. Marta stepped to Donna's side and wrapped an arm around her shoulders. James watched in awe as the child comforted the mother, the biological bond between them bridging the gap of so many lost years.

Donna reached to pull the walker in front of her. Marta helped position it so she could lean her full weight on it. "Should we go find a place for you to sit?"

"Yes, I do need to sit," Donna agreed. "And I have hardly let you get inside the door. I am so sorry!"

Marta kept a protective arm around her mother's shoulders as they headed for the front room. "No need to apologize," Marta replied. "There was no way to imagine how it would feel to meet each other this first time." She paused a moment and then continued, "And maybe now we have those tears out of the way, we can enjoy the rest of our time together!"

"Oh, I think there are lots more tears to come," Donna warned, "but I will try to save them for another time. I have waited for this moment far too long to spend it all weeping!"

Once seated, the two women spent a long minute looking at each other. From his perspective, James could not miss the striking resemblance that had not been obvious until they were side by side. Even in the little things—the shapes of their noses, their cheekbones, the way they held their heads—the miracle of life passed from one human to the next was adorned with fingerprints that could not be ignored. Without a doubt, Marta was the child of Donna!

"I gave up so much," Donna began, "but I am blessed to have this opportunity. Thank you for coming today."

Marta smiled. "We are fortunate," she agreed. "Sometimes, meetings like this are under unhappy terms. I have no ill will toward you at all. I grew up with parents who loved me very much."

Donna's eyes dropped to her hands in her lap. James could see her shoulders heave as she tried to hold her emotions at bay. "I am so relieved to hear you say that," she whispered.

Marta perched on the edge of her chair and leaned in, drawing their worlds together. "James has told me a little about your pregnancy—that your parents did not wish to be involved and would not allow James to be involved either. I can only imagine how difficult it was for you to go through all of it alone. I'm sure you realized you could not raise a child by yourself. Many young girls try, then make bad choices just to keep a roof over their heads. You did the right thing."

Marta reached to touch Donna's knee. Donna looked up again, tears brimming in her eyes. "Some would say I took the easy way out."

Marta's response was immediate. "Those people have no idea how you have agonized over your decision through the years. I would guess it has not been easy."

"The worst part was wondering what happened to you." Donna blinked back her tears. "Thanks to James, now I know." She turned to James with a renewed smile.

James nodded. "Yes, that was the worst part for me, too. Finding Marta and seeing how lovingly she was raised relieved the guilt I carried all those years."

"James tells me you have other children," Marta said. "I would like to hear about them."

Donna motioned for James to bring down the pictures from the fireplace mantel. He handed them to her one at a time as she introduced Marta to the rest of her family.

Donna spoke about Jack, Elizabeth, Kendra, and Andrew. Even though she freely answered questions and showed Marta the flowers Andrew had sent her, James sensed the heaviness in her heart and her hesitancy to share—especially when she spoke of Elizabeth.

Marta arranged the four picture frames on the table at her knees. "Thank you for telling me about your family," she said. She opened her purse and removed an envelope of pictures. "My turn to tell you about my family." She handed the first picture to Donna. "This is a photo of the couple who adopted me—my parents, Alice and David Jennings. My mother passed away almost a year ago, and I really miss her. Dad lives about three hours from me, so I don't see him very often. We try to talk every week, so I know he's doing okay. They farmed for a living, and my younger brother has now taken over most of the responsibility of the farm."

Donna took the photo and held it very tenderly in her hands. She stared into the faces of the two individuals she had tried to imagine for so many years. James watched her face as she studied the picture. What was she thinking? Was there resentment or gratitude? James prayed Donna would understand her difficult decision so many years ago had been the right one.

Tears slid down Donna's cheeks. She bowed her head, but there was no hiding the emotion the picture evoked. Marta glanced at James, her face drawn with concern. James could only nod. It was a moment Donna needed to get past, and the room grew quiet.

At last, Donna looked up, returning the picture to Marta. "Thank you, Marta, for sharing this picture with me. I have wondered about them for so very long!"

Marta tucked the picture at the bottom of the stack. "I just wanted to assure you the couple who adopted me were good people," she explained. "They truly loved me as if I were their own child."

Donna wiped at a tear. "The good outcome is more than I dared to imagine. I simply hoped you were fed and clothed."

Marta took Donna's hand and squeezed it. "I was very well cared for. My father and I still have a wonderful relationship." She handed a small stack of pictures to Donna. "I know James has shared pictures of Jannah already, but here are some he didn't have."

"Oh!" Donna exclaimed when she saw the young girl with her dog. "How is Tucker doing now?"

"James must have told you about Tucker's accident," Marta began. "That was a horrible experience for all of us! Fortunately, a very good veterinarian was at the right place when we needed him, and he was able to help Tucker recover and learn to walk with three legs. I don't know how Jannah would have coped if Tucker had not survived. They are inseparable! But Tucker can run and play almost as well as before, and Jannah loves him even more than before!"

"I am so happy it turned out well," Donna responded. She shifted to a picture of Jannah with a birthday cake. There were eight candles on the cake. "Is Jannah eight now?"

"Yes, this was taken at her last birthday," Marta replied. "She must be the same age as your granddaughter Kendra. I did not marry very young," she explained. "I was just fine on my own—until a young boy in my class convinced me his daddy needed a friend, and he was certain I was that friend." Marta's lips curved into a smile at the memory.

"So, you met the little boy's father and decided you were the friend he needed?" Donna guessed with a smile.

"We hit it off right away," Marta admitted. "Phil was the basketball coach, and he and Jake spent countless hours shooting baskets on our driveway court."

"Jake is Phil's son?" Donna asked.

"Yes, he was," Marta corrected. "They both died two years ago." The pain at the memory scratched across Marta's face.

"I'm sorry." Donna said nothing to betray James' confidence in her.

"It's okay," Marta assured her. "Jannah and I got through the dark days—with James' help. Jannah still has nightmares about parts of it but not as often as she did before. That was the worst part for me, knowing Jannah relived it over and over and over again."

"That would be very difficult for a mother," Donna agreed.

Marta handed her the next picture. "This is the school where I teach, and these are the kids I need to get to know better this year." She laughed softly. "It takes me a few days to match their names with their faces, and I'm not there yet with most of this bunch!"

"What grade do you teach?"

"Second grade right now," Marta answered. "I have always said I need the kids to be smart enough to understand what school is all about before I get them in my class. Second grade is just about right—they know the essentials of reading. I get to teach them how to put all their skills together to see how reading is used in math, and how math is used in science, and how science is used in everyday life. It is so much fun to see the lightbulbs go off in their little heads when they figure it all out!"

"Let's see," Donna mused out loud, "would Jannah be in second or third grade this year?"

"She is in third grade," Marta replied. "She wasn't in my class last year. Whenever possible, our principal sees that students don't have parents as teachers. I knew what she was studying last year, but she is on her own this year!"

James watched the two women thumb through more pictures, their heads leaning close together. It was as if they had forgotten he was in the room, and that pleased him. It was their moment, after all. Marta was their common denominator, and James enjoyed the opportunity to step back and watch them interact for the first time. It had not been a mistake to bring her. He had not misunderstood God's nudging.

CHAPTER TWENTY-THREE

DONNA SETTLED DOWN IN HER recliner and lifted her feet. What a day it had been! They had ordered a pizza for lunch and continued visiting around the table. Midafternoon, James announced that they should head home. Donna stood at the door, watching them pull away. When they were out of sight, the tears flowed again. It was so hard to let them go.

She reached for the Bible James had left many months ago. She still wondered if it was intentional, or did he really just forget it? Either way, Donna was certain it was God's plan. She had reluctantly picked it up and searched for the verses had James listed on the back page. The transformation those verses made in her life was undeniable. She had gone from a debilitated, hopeless invalid to an invigorated woman devoted to learning more about her Savior.

When she opened the Bible, the letter from Elizabeth slipped to her lap. Donna reached for it before it fell to the floor. She pulled the letter from the envelope and read it again. She hoped she had made the right decisions in telling Elizabeth and meeting Marta. But there was no undoing either one.

Her family *was* fragmented. But was it her fault? Had her husband found out about her first child somehow, and that caused him to be unfaithful to her? How would he have found out? She had been very careful to hide the only pieces of evidence she had—tiny footprints and a copy of the birth record.

It seemed unlikely to Donna her husband would have found out. Even if he had, would that excuse his behavior? The divorce caused more damage to his family than the secret of Marta. Was Elizabeth so angry with her she could not understand that? Was Donna now obliged to inform Elizabeth of Marta's visit today?

Marta! What a delightful woman! Beautiful and forgiving. There was nothing Donna had seen today that suggested Marta had experienced an unhappy childhood. For that, Donna was thankful. She was grateful to Marta's parents and grateful to God for providing. It was God, after all, Who had been at work in the situation, even though Donna had not had a relationship with Him at the time. He put David and Alice in the right spot at just the right time to be able to adopt her baby.

The letter dropped to her lap again as she leaned back and closed her eyes. She remembered the pictures of Jannah that Marta had shared. She even saw a few of Jannah's baby pictures. Marta understood how much Donna had missed and was willing to provide some pieces to the puzzle. Little Jannah suffered significant losses in the last two years, and Donna's heart ached at the thought. Those losses were Marta's as well. Again, Donna whispered a prayer of thanks to God for bringing James to comfort both Jannah and Marta.

Donna picked up the abandoned letter and read through it a second time. How was Donna supposed to respond to Elizabeth now? Maybe there would never be another opportunity to try to mend things with her. What if Marta returned home and decided meeting her biological mother was all she wished to do? What if she decided introducing Jannah to Donna would be too confusing for a child? What if both of her daughters chose to never speak to her again?

The only One Who understood the intricacies of all three women was the One Who had fashioned them in the womb. Donna bowed her head, sharing her burden with Him. "Dear God," she whispered, "please let me keep both my daughters. I love them both dearly. I'm not asking that they become friends—just that I can continue to love Elizabeth and begin to know Marta. Please heal the hurt I have caused Elizabeth and help her to forgive me." Donna paused before adding her last words of thanks. "And thank You for allowing my renewed friendship with James. You know I needed him. He knew I needed You. In Jesus' name I ask it all, amen."

When Donna opened her eyes, she looked around the room where she sat. Nothing had changed in her surroundings, but the peace in her heart swelled as she refolded the letter. She slid the letter back into the envelope and held it against her heart. *Ah, Elizabeth,* she thought. *You need to know God, too. I did not teach you about Him, but I hope I will have opportunities to demonstrate the peace He can bring!*

CHAPTER TWENTY-FOUR

MARTA DOZED IN THE SEAT for the last several miles. She jerked awake when the car stopped in her driveway. "James! I'm so sorry I could not stay awake to make sure you didn't fall asleep!" she said in a drowsy voice.

"No problem, Marta," James assured. "My mind has been busy while you slept. I really had no problem at all."

Marta reached over to pat his knee. "Thank you so much for going with me today," she said. "I would never have made this trip by myself."

James smiled. "I was glad to go along."

"I'm glad I went," Marta said. "I always thought I didn't need to know my biological parents. But after I found out you are my father, I've been wondering about my mother. I hope I helped convince her she made the right decision when I was born. I can't imagine the guilt she has been living with all these years!"

"Guilt is a brutal task master," James acknowledged. "It is a force that overshadows every thought. It destroys a person's self-esteem. It eats away at any joy in life. And it makes a person question every decision they make." James shook his head, as if chasing away private memories of guilt's devastation. "Thank you for being willing to put Donna's mind at ease." He laid his hand over Marta's before she opened the car door.

"Thanks again," Marta replied. "Now, get home and get some sleep!" She jumped out of the car and headed for the front door. She knew James would sit in the driveway until she was safely inside. She turned to wave at him before closing the door behind her.

The quietness of the house felt odd. Even though Jannah and Tucker were spending another night at Pat's house, Marta tiptoed down the hall and peeked into the room where she tucked her daughter into bed every night. She smiled at the sight of pajamas in a pile by Jannah's bed. The bedspread was haphazardly pulled up. The collection of stuffed animals that shared Jannah's bed at night huddled together near her pillow. The room was filled with the smell of a young girl, and Marta breathed in deep, enjoying it all.

The rocking chair where she had cradled baby Jannah to sleep still sat in the corner of the room. A few clothes had been tossed in the seat, but Marta pushed them aside and relaxed into the familiarity of the wooden arms. What a day it had been! She should be climbing into bed, getting the sleep she had wished upon James, but the emotional rush still pumped through her veins. She leaned back in the chair and began the soothing rock.

Donna really was nothing at all like Marta had imagined. James had told her about Donna's stroke, but Marta was still surprised to see her mother depending upon a walker to get around. She seemed much older than James, but they were the same age.

Even when Donna was telling Marta about her other children, there was a lonely tone to her voice. It did not sound like the children came to visit very often. The one son seemed to call frequently, but a phone call could never replace the presence of a child. Though Donna lovingly introduced each child to her, her voice lacked the enthusiasm a mother should have.

As for her own child, Marta wondered how she should answer Jannah's questions about the trip she had taken with Grandpa Hawkeye. Jannah would want to meet her grandmother! But she had experienced so much loss and death already. Would getting attached to an elderly woman make life harder for Jannah in the future? On the other hand, Marta knew Jannah would bring so much joy to Donna's life. How could she deny Donna that relationship?

Tonight was not the time for those decisions. Marta stood and headed toward her own bedroom. Her steps were suddenly heavy with exhaustion. She slipped into her pajamas and collapsed onto her bed. The thought of seeing Jannah in the morning curled her lips into a smile. Pat would be there, too!

THE NEXT MORNING, TUCKER ANNOUNCED Marta's arrival, and Jannah was right behind him. Marta held her arms wide and pulled her daughter close. Their short separation ended in a hug sprinkled with much laughter.

"Mom, I missed you!" Jannah whispered when their hearts were connected.

"I missed you, too, Jannah!" Marta replied in her daughter's ear. She pushed her daughter back so she could see the smile on the girl's freckled face.

"You are going to have to tell me all about your trip," Jannah said.

"And you are going to have to tell me all about your time at the clinic," Marta countered. "But first, I need to thank Pat for taking care of you and Tucker while I was away."

"Come on in," Jannah invited. "Dr. Pat is in the kitchen fixing breakfast for us. We have already been to the clinic to feed the pets. Now, it's time for our breakfast!"

"Well, it sounds like I arrived at the perfect time."

"Yes, you did! Dr. Pat really knows how to cook!" Jannah took her hand and lead her to the kitchen.

Pat leaned against the sink. "Hey there, Marta! I figured it must be you, the way Tucker was carrying on. I hope you haven't had breakfast yet. There is plenty here for you to join us."

Marta's heart felt full as she stood in the room with her daughter, Tucker, and the man who had become such a good friend. "It certainly smells yummy," she responded. "And no, I haven't had breakfast—my house was so quiet, I had to come right away to reclaim my noisemakers!"

"Good!" Pat answered. "The egg casserole will be ready in about five minutes. I will put you and Jannah to work setting the table." He handed them a stack of paper plates and plasticware. "We're going to use my fine china!" he teased.

"Perfect!" Marta said. "Lead the way, Jannah!" The pair headed into the dining room and placed the settings around the small table. Marta glanced into the next room. A lamp beside a large recliner brightened the living room. A plaid blanket was folded and draped over the end of the couch. On the floor by the couch, Tucker's basket of toys from home was filled and ready for play. Everything seemed to be in its place. Was it always so tidy, or was it because Pat was expecting her this morning?

"There's a fruit bowl in the fridge. Juice, too," Pat called from the kitchen. "I am taking the casserole out of the oven, so stand back!" Marta scooted back to give him room to carry the hot dish to the table.

"What's so funny?" Pat asked as he passed her. A potholder was tucked under his elbow, and a dish towel hung over his shoulder. He slapped the potholder onto the table and placed the steaming casserole on it.

"What do you mean?" Marta responded with a quizzed look on her face.

"You had a silly grin on your face just now. How come?"

Heat rushed to Marta's face. "Oh, well, I was just thinking how I would not have guessed you to be so domesticated." She giggled at the word that had fallen out of her mouth.

"Really?" Pat pretended to be offended. "There might be a lot of things you don't know about me!" His laughter filled the dining room.

"Any bigger surprises than this?" Marta asked, spreading her arms wide to encompass the table before them.

Pat winked at her. "Maybe you should stick around and find out!"

"I might do that!" Marta countered.

"I'd like that," Pat responded, his words quieter and intended for Marta alone. He turned to include Jannah again. "Now, let's see if this breakfast is fit to eat!"

"DON'T FORGET YOUR SHOES AT the back door!" Pat called to Jannah as she gathered up her bag of clothes.

"Got 'em already!"

Marta and Pat were in the kitchen finishing up the dishes from breakfast.

"So, your trip went well?" Pat asked.

"It did!" Marta answered. "My mother was not at all what I expected, but she was very pleasant—and I think meeting me was something she never even dared to hope for. I know now her decision to place me for adoption was not easy."

"Do you think you will see her again?" Pat pulled the dish towel from his shoulder and dried his hands after draining the sink.

Marta hung her damp towel over the oven handle. "I know she wants to meet Jannah. I'm not sure yet how I feel about that."

"Give yourself some time to think about it," Pat advised. "Jannah's life has been pretty complicated the last couple years."

"That's true," Marta agreed. She looked around the kitchen to make sure they had not missed a dirty dish. "We need to get out of here and let you have a little peace and quiet before the whole weekend is over. Thank you again for letting Jannah hang out with you. And Tucker, too!"

Pat stacked the last dish back into the cupboard. "They were no trouble at all—great company for me, in fact!" Pat pulled Marta into a hug. "Glad to have you home, though!" he whispered into her ear.

Marta leaned into the arms that held her. It felt so comfortable, so right to be close to him. She breathed in the spicy cologne on his neck. She felt his soft breath tickle her neck. She closed her eyes, imagining what life might be like if—

"Mom, are you ready to go?" Jannah's voice called from the next room. And then, she appeared in the doorway. A puzzled look crossed her face as she viewed the two of them so close together.

Pat tightened one arm around her as they turned to face Jannah. It was too late to hide their affection. His voice remained positive and reassuring. "I was just thanking your mom for helping with the breakfast cleanup." Pat pulled the damp dish towel from his shoulder and tossed it on the counter.

"But it is time to go," Marta sputtered as she stepped away from Pat. She crossed her arms in front of her and cocked her head toward Jannah. "Do you have all your things together? Tucker's, too?"

"Yes." Jannah frowned. "We've been waiting on you."

"Right behind you!" Marta followed Jannah out of the kitchen, shooting a perplexed look over her shoulder toward Pat. "Tell Pat thanks for letting you stay."

Jannah didn't look back as she walked. "Thanks," she muttered.

Marta bit back the reproach rising to her lips. She turned to look at Pat and shrugged her shoulders, silently apologizing for her daughter's impolite response.

Pat waved her on with an understanding grin. "See you later," he called after them. "And thanks for your help at the clinic, Jannah!"

"Sure," the girl replied as she grabbed her bags and headed out the door.

"I could carry some of that for you," Marta offered.

"I've got it," Jannah answered. "Come on, Tucker." The two of them climbed into the car, and she pulled the door shut with an angry thud.

Marta turned again to find Pat leaning against the door frame, a smile on his face as he waved to her. *Easy for him to grin,* she thought. *He doesn't have to explain to Jannah what just happened in his kitchen!* Marta settled into the driver's seat and put the car in gear.

"Everything go okay while I was gone?" she asked after she pulled out onto the street.

"I guess so."

Marta looked in her rearview mirror. Jannah was slumped against Tucker. The dog sat tall in the seat, his tongue hanging out as his head turned every direction, keeping track of all the cars darting past them. Whatever had Jannah so upset had no effect on Tucker.

"Did you enjoy helping at the clinic?"

"It was okay."

Marta glanced in the mirror again. Helping at the clinic was the one thing Jannah had been most excited about when she heard she would get to spend a night with Pat.

"Just okay?" Marta pressed.

"It was," Jannah repeated. "I really don't want to talk about it right now."

Marta drove on in silence. Jannah had been so excited to see her only a couple hours ago, and now there was nothing but icy silence between them. It was the hug. It was the surprise of seeing her mother touching another man. They should have been more guarded. This was not like years ago when her husband's son decided he wanted his daddy and his teacher to like each other. Jannah was not at that place yet. It was still too soon after her daddy had died. Marta's heart ached for her.

Marta pulled into the driveway and pushed the button to open the garage door. She put the car in park and leaned back in the driver's seat. She needed a moment to calm her mind. Jannah pushed her door open and called for Tucker to follow her. She grabbed her overnight bag and slammed the door shut. Marta watched her daughter in the rearview mirror as she stomped into the house.

Finally, Marta gathered her purse and opened the car door. A deep sigh escaped her lips as she made her way toward the house. There would have to be some conversation with Jannah about her friendship with Pat, but what exactly would she say? That she would deny her own feelings and end the friendship if that was what Jannah wanted? Would Jannah ask that much?

Marta walked through the kitchen and settled down in her recliner. Out of the corner of her eye, she saw Jannah's bedroom door was closed. Maybe they both needed some time alone before they talked. She put her feet up and closed her eyes. Sleep was a welcome escape.

Jannah rolled to her back on her bed, listening for any sounds on the other side of her closed door. Tucker stood to monitor her movement, then rested his head on her arm.

"Oh, Tucker!" Jannah whispered. "Why did you have to go and get hurt, anyway?" She turned to her side and patted the dog's head. Tucker looked at her, his big, brown eyes begging for forgiveness.

"If you hadn't gotten hurt, we would never have met Dr. Pat," she continued. "And you would still have four legs!" Jannah allowed a sniffle. "Why did all this have to happen?"

The sniffle gave way to tears, and soon, she was sobbing into her pillow. Her shoulders shook with the weight of her despair. What could be worse than her mommy falling in love with Dr. Pat? Something horrible would happen to him, and then Mommy would be so sad all over again! And if something horrible happened to Dr. Pat, she wasn't sure she would ever get over it.

Jannah reached to pull Tucker close. He licked her face, wiping away the tears. She buried her face in the warmth of the dog's neck. "I love you so much, Tucker! Please don't ever, ever, ever leave me!"

CHAPTER TWENTY-FIVE

DONNA WOKE TO FIND THE sun peeking through the curtains in her bedroom window. She must have overslept if the sun was so bright already! She looked around the room and gathered her wits before throwing the blankets back.

Last night, she had decided to call Elizabeth first thing in the morning. It was not a call she looked forward to. Elizabeth was angry, and Donna would be defensive. She knew she would need to speak carefully.

She pushed her toes into the slippers by her bed and stood slowly. The walker was only a foot away, and she reached to pull it close. Suddenly, a horrible pain ripped through Donna's head. She collapsed onto the floor and wrapped her arms around her throbbing head. Then, there was just silent darkness.

Donna wasn't sure how many hours passed before she was able to touch the call button on her wrist. She remembered darkness, but all the while, she heard the faint ticking of the grandfather clock in the front room. She wanted to shout for help, but her lips would not open. Finally, she willed her fingers to search for the help button.

"Donna, this is Emergency Care. Can you hear me?" Again, Donna tried to respond, but no words came.

"Donna, can you hear me?" The emergency response team member repeated her question, her words now weighted with concern.

"Donna, do you need help?"

Donna could not open her eyes. She could not move to push her leg into a more comfortable position on the floor. But this time, she was able to whisper a simple, "Yes!"

"I will dispatch the EMTs immediately."

The key to the door was tucked in the back of the mailbox, and instructions to find the key were included in her emergency plan with the hospital. Donna licked her dry lips with a thick tongue and then allowed oblivion to end her thoughts.

Minutes later, sounds of the EMTs moving quietly through the house stirred Donna's weak awareness. They called out her name, but she could not answer. They would look in every room and eventually would find her. At last, steps entered her bedroom. She felt them straighten her body on the floor with gentle hands. They placed a pillow under her head. They unzipped bags and pulled out their equipment. Soon, a blood pressure cuff tightened around her arm. An oximeter was clipped to her finger. They kept saying her name, begging for a response of some kind.

Donna listened as they radioed the hospital. She heard the gurney snap into place as they lowered it to the floor. They lifted her body to the gurney and covered her with layers of blankets. She felt the warmth of the sun on her face as they rolled her to the ambulance. Still the curtain of darkness separated her from consciousness.

There was something familiar about it all. The hushed voices reporting her vitals. The bumps and turns as the ambulance hurried toward the emergency room. The sound of the door being pulled open. The rapid transfers and cold hands working to connect her to beeping monitors. She felt her heart race and then halt for an eternity, then race again. Her head ached beyond words. Could death be worse?

Suddenly, there were no voices and no beeping. Just complete darkness.

Marta woke with a start. She froze in place, straining her ears. All was quiet in the house. Something had awakened her, though, and her body tingled with the sensation. She inched to a sitting position and pushed the covers away from her. Had Jannah left the house for some reason? It was later than Marta normally awoke, but the night had been a restless one filled with worries about her daughter.

She poked her toes into her slippers and fluffed her hair with her fingers. Something had happened to wake her. The thought made Marta uneasy. She opened her bedroom door and crept down the hallway to Jannah's door. It was still shut. Marta tapped lightly on the door and then opened it a crack. Tucker stood and came to the door.

Jannah was sprawled across her bed, her covers clinging to the mattress haphazardly. Marta smiled when she saw a bare foot dangling over the edge. Jannah and her daddy had called the exposed foot their "radiators," intended to keep their body temperatures on an even keel.

Jannah did not stir. Marta opened the door wider; and Tucker wiggled his way out, his tail wagging a morning greeting. He headed for the door, and Marta followed to let him outside. She stood at the door and watched to make sure the dog didn't leave the yard. His imaginary leash was much shorter after the accident.

Marta again wondered what had awakened her. Was it just a noisy vehicle? That was seldom an issue, since the main road was two blocks away. She couldn't explain it, but she felt like something had alerted her. She shook her shoulders to chase away the feeling. Jannah and Tucker were both safe. She must have imagined the eerie feeling.

Tucker raced to the door opened for him. He stopped at Marta's feet and wagged his tail. It was time for his morning treat, and Marta did not disappoint him. She patted his head as he crunched the morsel. Satisfied, he curled up in the warm sun by the deck doors.

Marta settled down in her recliner and opened an abandoned magazine. If Jannah could sleep longer, Marta would do what she could to keep the house quiet. James usually offered to give them a ride to his church, but Marta usually declined. Sundays were her unscheduled days, and the prospect of sitting there doing absolutely nothing for an hour was intoxicating!

The vibrating cell phone in her pocket startled her. Marta fished it out and smiled when she saw the call was from Pat.

"Hi, Pat," she answered in a whisper.

"Hey!" he responded. "Why are you whispering?"

"Jannah is still sleeping, and I'm trying to keep it quiet for her."

"Oh!" Pat replied. "Well, speaking of Jannah, I need to apologize for my part in what she saw yesterday. It was pretty obvious she was shocked to see us so close."

"Yes, she was," Marta agreed. A deep sigh escaped her worried heart.

"I'm sorry I was careless. It was just so good to see you, and I enjoyed having you join us for breakfast. But I didn't stop to think how Jannah might feel about it." Pat's voice cracked. "I am sorry, Marta."

"I know. I didn't think about Jannah's feelings either. She was very cool toward me on the way home, and she went straight to her room and closed the door behind her."

There was a long pause before Pat responded. "Do you think I need to keep my distance for a while? I don't want to do anything to make life difficult for either of you!"

"I-I don't know," Marta stammered. "Maybe for a little while. Maybe she will talk to me about it today." Marta could feel the disappointment in Pat's silence. Her heart raced in opposite directions—to protect her daughter and to shield the budding affection for this man who had begun to fill a deep void in her life.

"Okay," Pat whispered. "Let me know if I can do anything to help." The distance swelled between them. "Marta, I'm going to miss you. Call me when you can, please."

"I will, Pat. I will miss you, too!" She ended the call and crumbled back in her chair to let the tears fall.

The steaming coffee in James' cup sloshed from side to side when the phone in his pocket startled him. He set down the cup and reached for his phone, wondering whose name would pop up on the screen. It was a number he didn't recognize, but it came from Donna's hometown.

"Hello?"

"Hello. Is this James Hawthorne?"

"Yes, I am James. Can I help you?"

"This is the Broadlawns Hospital in Riverton. We have a patient in intensive care, and her emergency directives included informing you of any hospitalization. Her name is Donna Wright. Do you know her?"

James' throat constricted. "Yes. Yes, I know Donna," he stammered. "What happened?" A chill crawled across the back of his neck.

"She was brought to the ER by ambulance early this morning," the caller said. "It appears she has suffered a stroke. We have stabilized her and moved her to our intensive care unit. She has an emergency response service through us, and your name is on the list of people to contact."

James closed his eyes and leaned his head back on his chair. Not again! How could this be happening to Donna all over again? "Has her family been contacted as well?" James asked.

"Some of them have been contacted. We have not been able to reach her daughter yet. We were wondering if you might know of an alternative number to try."

Elizabeth! James had no phone number for her. He had never imagined needing one. "I'm sorry. No, I don't have another number for her. Have you made contact with Donna's two sons?"

"Yes," the caller responded. "We spoke directly with Andrew. He is several states away, but he said he will come this way immediately. We were only able to leave a message for Jack to return our call. His commanding officer is to get the message to him right away."

"So, there is no one there with Donna right now?" James asked.

"That is correct," came the reply.

"Is she conscious?" James almost whispered the question.

"She's sleeping. We don't have test results yet. We just wanted to contact people Donna had listed on her directives. Do you know where the hospital is located?"

"I have not been there before, but I'm sure I can find it," James replied. "I will make some arrangements here at home and be there by this afternoon." He looked around the room, making a mental list of things he needed to do. "Thank you for calling me. And if Donna does awaken, please let her know I am coming."

"I will pass on those instructions," the caller assured him.

James disconnected the call and let the phone fall to his lap. Where was God's timing in this? Second strokes are often fatal or, at least, more debilitating. Donna had just met Marta and was hoping to meet Jannah soon. Why would God allow this?

It was time to pray. It was time to pour out his heart at the feet of the One Who was in control of all life—time to seek comfort from the One Who knew the end of the story.

James abandoned the cooled coffee and retreated to the rocker by his bed. He held his head in his hands and let the tears flow. Between sobs, he whispered his prayer. "Dear God, please be with Donna. Thank You for showing yourself to her in the pages of an old Bible. Thank You for healing the painful scars of her past. Thank You for granting her the pleasure of meeting her firstborn daughter." The sobs overtook James until his chest heaved. There was one more thing he must ask of his God. "Please let me get there soon enough."

James leaned back into the comfort of the rocker. He considered sharing the news with Marta. Would she want to go with him? Or would she just feel obligated to accompany him? Was there even time to give Marta the choice?

James pulled open the closet and reached for the overnight bag he had tucked away the night before. How could he have known that within hours he would be filling it again? He moved the razor over the night's stubble and then reached for his toothbrush. He pushed the shower curtain aside and turned on the water. There was not a lot of time left to make the call to Marta if he was going to.

Just as James stepped into the shower, his cell phone rang. He froze in place, afraid to even look at the display. It could be the hospital telling him he did not need to make the trip after all because Donna had passed. The ringing continued, and he finally had to pick up the phone. It was Marta!

"Hey, James, this is Marta," she whispered. "Is everything okay?"

James shoulders heaved. *Was* everything okay? "Hi, Marta," he answered.

"I woke this morning with the oddest feeling that something is not right," Marta continued. "Are you okay?"

James reached for his towel and wrapped it around him. He slumped down on the toilet seat. "Oh, Marta," he began with another heavy sigh, "I just got a call from a hospital in the town where Donna lives. They think she has had another stroke. My name is on her emergency contact list, so they called to see if I could come to be with her."

"No!" Marta exclaimed. "How could that be? We were just with her!"

"I know," James agreed. "The hospital staff tried to get ahold of Donna's children. One son is on his way, but he is hundreds of miles away with his job. The other son is on a naval ship somewhere, and they couldn't even get ahold of Donna's daughter at all. I think I need to go."

A long moment passed before Marta spoke. "Well, I am her daughter, too, and I think I need to go as well. Do you mind?"

"Definitely not!" The burden lifted from his heart. "I was just debating whether or not to call you. I didn't want you to feel like you had to go." He halted before voicing the fact that threatened his calm. "You know, second strokes are very often fatal. Donna might not survive this one."

"Then I do need to go," Marta replied without hesitation. "How soon were you planning to leave? I will need to make some arrangements for Jannah. I'm not sure she will want to stay with Pat again—there was sort of an incident when I picked her up yesterday."

"Really?" Surprise ricocheted in James' head. "I thought Jannah and Pat were best of friends!"

"It's a long story." Marta sighed. "I will tell you about it later. I need to get moving if I am going with you. What time shall we shoot for?"

"I can be ready in less than an hour, but I know it will take longer than that for you," James answered. "When can you be ready?"

"Would ten o'clock be okay?"

"That's fine. I will go gas up the car while I'm waiting." He stepped back into the shower and flipped on the water, relieved that the decision to tell Marta had been made for him.

CHAPTER TWENTY-SIX

MARTA SLIPPED HER PHONE BACK into her pocket and looked at Tucker. "Now, what am I going to do?" she asked the oblivious animal. Tucker stood and padded to her side. Marta put her hands around his jowls and scratched behind his ears. "Tucker, what should I do?" she repeated. He cocked his head as if in thought.

"There's only one thing I can do," Marta resolved. She gave Tucker one last scratch, then stood to put her plan into motion. "Jannah is going with me. And you are going back to Pat!" She slipped out the deck door and selected Pat's number from the contacts list on her phone. When he answered, Marta shared the news about her mother.

"Can Tucker stay with you again?" She tried to mask the hesitancy in her voice.

"Of course, he can! Jannah, too?"

"No, I'm taking her with me." There was no hesitancy now. "It might be the only chance she has to see my mother."

"Are you sure you want to do that?" Pat queried. "You just met your mother yourself."

"Oh, I know, Pat! Please don't make me think about this too much," Marta begged. "If I do, I might change my mind. Then I might be sorry later. I'm trying to make the right decision without much time to dwell on the consequences."

"Okay, Marta." Pat's voice softened. "Jannah has a very tender heart. If she knows how much this means to you, she will want to be with you."

"I think so, too," Marta agreed. "But it is happening at a bad time. Jannah is upset with me right now. I don't know how she will handle all the puzzle pieces I am going to have to share with her on our way to the hospital."

"Just be honest with her," Pat advised. "James will be there for Jannah—you know that."

"Yes, he's always there for Jannah." Marta relaxed in the assurance of James' support. "So, I'll bring Tucker by in a couple hours, okay?"

"Okay. I'll be looking for you!" Pat grew quiet. "And, Marta? I'll be thinking about you. I hope your mother recovers and has the chance to get to know Jannah. It would be a shame if she only gets to say goodbye."

James pulled into Marta's driveway at ten sharp. He rested his head against the seat and took advantage of the opportunity for a quick prayer.

"Dear God, thank You for helping Marta make the decision to go with me. I ask that You give Donna more time with this child, but I know Your plan is best and good. Help me to say and do the things that are most helpful."

James opened his eyes at the sound of the house door opening. Marta, Jannah, and Tucker were headed toward the car. James hopped out to help load the luggage into the trunk.

As soon as James' feet touched the ground, Tucker was beside him for the expected greeting. James petted the dog's head, scratching behind his ears. Tucker's tail wagged with glee.

"How ya doin', Tucker?" James asked as the dog tilted his head sideways to accommodate more ear-scratching. Tucker's tongue dangled out the side of his mouth, and he panted his pleasure.

"I think he is terribly excited to see you and to go see Dr. Pat again!" Marta observed as she handed the luggage to James.

James hefted the bags into his trunk. "So, it worked out for Pat to keep Tucker again?"

"Oh, yes! Tucker is very spoiled to have so many people who love him! Dr. Pat is just one more!"

James turned to greet Jannah, but she turned away and kicked at a rock. Now was not the time to question her heart; so James shut the trunk lid, and they all found their places in his car. It was a quiet ride across town. The morning phone call had dampened the day's tone, but James sensed there was more to it than that.

Pat was at his door when they pulled into his driveway. Tucker's head perked up as if on cue, and his tail swatted Jannah's chest.

"Go!" Jannah ordered as she opened the car door to release Tucker. The dog bounded over the girl's lap and took off in his lopsided, three-legged gait. Pat squatted down to meet him.

Marta followed Tucker up the sidewalk. "I guess Tucker thought he would never see you again!" She laughed. Pat grinned at her, nothing on his face masking the pleasure he took in seeing her.

James waited for Jannah to climb out of the car, but she just sat there looking down at her feet. Marta jumped back into the front seat and fastened her seatbelt. Confused, James backed out of Pat's driveway. He turned to look at Marta with eyes that begged an explanation.

"She's going with us," Marta mouthed silently. James glanced into the rearview mirror and saw Jannah's face pressed against the window as they drove away from Tucker.

"Oh!" He nodded in silent patience.

The car picked up speed after they pulled onto the interstate. James set the cruise control and lifted his eyes to the mirror to check on Jannah again. Her head was laid back against the seat, and her eyes were closed. Maybe she was sleeping. So many questions swirled in his heart, but he dared not ask them yet.

Marta must have heard his gentle sigh. She turned to look at him; then she looked back at Jannah. "You asleep, Jannah?" she asked in a whisper.

"Nope," Jannah replied.

"Can we talk a little?" Marta asked. There was a tender plea in her voice.

"Might as well," Jannah answered as she opened her eyes and sat up in the seat. The chill in her voice warned all was not well between the daughter and her mother.

Marta pulled one leg up into the seat, and she turned to face Jannah as much as her seatbelt would allow. "I need to explain to you where we are going," she began. She sucked in a deep breath before continuing. "Grandpa Hawkeye got a call in the night from a hospital quite a ways from here. They told him someone we know was brought there by ambulance and is not doing very well."

Jannah leaned toward her mother and tilted her head in keen attention. "Who is it?"

"Well, you don't know her yet, but I would like you to meet her." Marta swallowed her apprehension and continued. "It is my mother— my biological mother."

"What do you mean, your 'biological mother'?"

James lifted his eyes to the rearview mirror and saw Jannah's confused face. He reached over and patted Marta's knee. It was all the encouragement he could offer. This conversation had to remain between Marta and her daughter.

"You know I was adopted as a baby, right?" Marta quizzed.

"Yes, you told me that." Jannah's eyebrows pinched together in thought. "But you said you didn't know her."

"I didn't at that time," Marta replied. "While Grandpa Hawkeye and I were gone over the weekend, I met her for the first time."

"Was she sick?" Jannah pushed herself back into the seat with the tip of her toe, then stretched against the seatbelt toward her mother.

"Not sick, but she is recovering from a stroke. It takes a long time to get over a stroke."

"Why didn't you just tell me you were going to see her?" Confusion shadowed Jannah's face as she shook her head. "I wondered where you went, and Dr. Pat didn't want to talk about it."

"I'm sorry for not being more open with you, Jannah. It's just that I wasn't sure how I myself felt about meeting my mother for the first time." Marta turned to look at Jannah, meeting her eyes in a silent plea for understanding.

"So, is she the one who is in the hospital now?"

"Yes."

"Is she going to . . . die?" Jannah's voice trembled as she uttered the dreaded word.

Marta turned further in her seat, reaching to touch Jannah's knee. "I don't know, but I would like you to meet her before she does die. You are her granddaughter, and she wants to know you."

Jannah leaned back in her seat and looked out the side window. James lifted his eyes to the mirror and saw the child's clinched jawline. How he wished he could park the car and wrap them both in his arms! His responsibility for this moment weighed heavily on him.

"I don't even know her!" Jannah sputtered under her breath. "Why does she want to know me? What difference will it make if she meets me? Especially if she is going to die?"

"That is hard to explain," Marta answered. "Could you trust me and believe we are doing the right thing today? My mother is a very patient woman, who has waited many years for the opportunity to meet a child she never knew."

"Why aren't you mad at her for giving you away?" Jannah's face turned back to her mother, and there was bewilderment written all over it.

"Well, Jannah, that question is easy to explain," Marta replied. "I am a mother, and I understand the natural desire to do what is best for my child. My biological mother felt she was doing what was best for me when she allowed me to be adopted. She chose to give me the chance for a better life than she could give me herself."

James peeked into the rearview mirror again. Jannah sat with her arms crossed in front of her. Her lips were pursed in childish contemplation of the maternal insight her mother had shared. How could a child understand a decision a mother makes in a situation like Marta described? Marta was right; Jannah would either trust her decision or not.

"What is her name?"

"Donna Wright," Marta answered.

"Where does she live?"

"About five hours from our house, so it's going to take a while yet to get there." Marta turned again to add an encouraging smile to her answer.

"So, that is why we brought overnight bags?"

"Yes. We don't know how long we might stay."

Jannah squirmed in her seat and leaned her head back. "I wish Tucker could have come, too," she said.

Marta offered a tender smile. "Maybe when my mother goes home, we can bring Tucker another time. I'm positive she would love him."

"He knows how it feels to almost die," Jannah whispered.

Marta startled at the reminder of Tucker's accident. Jannah seldom mentioned it. Almost dying? Yes, Marta knew that feeling, too. She turned her face to the window to hide her threatening tears.

CHAPTER TWENTY-SEVEN

JAMES DROPPED MARTA AND JANNAH off at the hospital entrance, then pulled the car into the closest parking spot. For a brief moment, he wrapped his arms around the steering wheel and begged God to help him through the coming hours. He grabbed his jacket and hurried to the entrance. Inside, he ushered the mother and daughter to the information desk.

"May I help you?" the elderly lady asked.

What a job hers would be, James thought, *to be face-to-face with so many distraught families each day!* "We would like to visit Donna Wright," he replied softly.

"Let me find her room number." The clerk dipped her head toward a computer screen and tapped on a directory. "Here we go. She is on the fourth floor in room 405. Her visits are limited to fifteen minutes with family only." She raised her eyes again. "Do you know where the elevators are located?"

"No, we don't," James answered.

The clerk rolled away from her desk and motioned toward the corridor on her left, verbally navigating them through the steps to Donna's room. James thanked the woman and directed Marta and Jannah to follow him down the long hallway. A bright sign pointed them to the elevators. James sensed their collective sigh of unease as they waited for the doors to slide open.

Jannah stepped into the elevator with wide eyes. James watched her face as the upward movement caught the girl's breath. It was such a simple thing—riding on an elevator. Still, it was something Jannah had not often experienced. She hung onto the wooden railing until the car stopped.

They approached a nurses' station on the fourth floor. It was the hub of activity for the area, the checkpoint for all who brought comfort for loved ones. The nurses' quiet chatter ceased as the three visitors approached.

"Can we help you?"

"We are here to visit Donna Wright," James answered. "I believe she is in room 405. Is this a good time for us to see her?"

"Are you family?"

"Yes, we are."

"Good! It will be good for Donna to see some familiar faces. Let me take you in." She came from around the counter and motioned for them to follow her. "We ask you limit your visit to fifteen minutes," she said as she stopped at Donna's door. "She needs all the rest she can get, but she also needs to see people she loves. The doctor's orders are for one visitor at a time, but this first time, you can all go in for just a few minutes."

The nurse pushed open the door and took measure of her patient's status. "Donna, you have some visitors," she announced in a soft voice. There was no response from Donna. The nurse turned to James and explained, "She has been medicated to keep her from restless stirring, but I think she will hear you if you talk to her. Don't be disappointed if she can't respond."

James moved toward the bed and lifted Donna's limp hand into his own. He wrapped his fingers around the warm hand, hoping for a soft squeeze in return. There was none, but he kept the lifeless hand tucked into his. For a moment, he forgot the others in the room with them. As his eyes studied her face, he saw the teenage girl who had captured his heart so many years ago—his first love. He didn't feel the physical attraction of their youth, but instead, he felt emotional investment that young lovers expend so casually. Their casual love had brought them to this moment in time.

"Donna," he whispered, "this is James." Tears welled in his eyes. "I brought two ladies you will be happy to see. Marta and Jannah are here." He blinked back the tears before he moved to offer his place to the visitors behind him.

Marta stepped forward and took her mother's hand. James watched as her eyes searched Donna's face for any sign of recognition. Marta tried to speak, but emotions choked out her words. After a moment, Marta's thoughts came tumbling out of her full heart.

"Donna, this is Marta," she began. "I want you to know that I am here, and I brought your granddaughter to meet you. I had wondered if there would ever be an opportunity for you to meet Jannah, and here we are!"

Marta stepped back and took Jannah's hand, coaxing her closer to the bedside. Side by side, they stood next to the woman who had given them life, separated by a generation and years of missed opportunities. Marta wrapped her arm around the young girl's shoulders and pulled her close.

"This is Jannah, your granddaughter," Marta whispered. "I will describe her to you: She is the most beautiful thing that ever happened to me. She is eight years old, and she has the prettiest blue eyes! Sometimes, her brown hair is pulled back into an easy ponytail; and sometimes, it just does whatever it wants to do. She has a dog she loves as much as life, and his name is Tucker. She even wanted to bring him today so you could meet him as well."

Jannah laughed nervously at the mention of Tucker. "He would have his nose on your pillow saying 'hello,'" Jannah added softly. "I hope that wouldn't bother you." Jannah relaxed and set her hand on the side of the bed.

"Bring him . . . next time." Donna suddenly spoke without opening her eyes. The response was a struggle, spoken in broken but clear words.

James rushed to the bed and stood behind Marta as they all waited for more. There was no movement, only the slightest rise of Donna's chest as she breathed. Had they imagined her response to Jannah? Marta turned questioning eyes to James. He lifted his shoulders and cocked his head toward Donna.

"Keep talking," he mouthed.

"Jannah, tell Donna what happened to Tucker," Marta encouraged.

Jannah swallowed hard. She looked at her mother, who nodded her head to tell the story. "Tucker went chasing a rabbit, and he got into the road. Someone hit him on the road. It took me a few minutes to find him. I called and called to him, but he didn't come like he always does. Then I heard him crying and found him on the road."

Jannah sucked in a deep breath. "I started running to Tucker. Then I saw a man kneeling down beside him on the road and talking to him and petting his nose. It was Dr. Pat. We took Tucker to Dr. Pat's office, and he helped Tucker get better. Now, Tucker can run and play on three legs as good as he could before." Jannah paused, considering how much to share. "Well, he is a little wobbly, but he doesn't let that slow him down!"

"I . . . know." Again, the lifeless lips spoke to the young girl. The three visitors froze at the sound of the woman's voice.

Jannah looked at her mother, her eyebrows arched in surprise. "How does she know all about Tucker?"

James patted Jannah's shoulders. "She always asks about you. I told her about Tucker's accident."

A nurse entered with a soft knock. "We need to let Donna rest," she advised. "You are welcome to wait in the chapel and then come one at a time to spend a few more minutes with her."

"Please stay," the quiet plea was loud enough for the nurse to hear.

The nurse looked at the clock. "How about if just one of you stays here with Donna?"

"Jan-nah," came the labored voice from the bed.

The three adults looked at the young girl. Her eyes went wide; but she shrugged, and then a self-confident smile washed across her face. "I will stay," Jannah answered without hesitation.

"Are you sure?" Marta questioned.

"Yep," Jannah replied. The nurse slid a chair close to the bedside and motioned for Jannah to have a seat.

James bent close to Donna's face. "Marta and I will be back in a little bit," he assured her. He motioned for Marta to follow him and the nurse out into the hallway. Marta glanced over her shoulder at the daughter she was leaving behind.

CHAPTER TWENTY-EIGHT

JANNAH SETTLED INTO THE CHAIR next to the hospital bed. She looked around the room at the machines humming softly in the background. A whiteboard announced the nurse's name for the current shift was Sandy. The window blind was pulled down most of the way, but Jannah could see a few clouds in the sky from the narrow opening.

Feeling like a spy, Jannah snuck a look at the old woman's face. There were lots of wrinkles, but Jannah could imagine she had been a pretty woman. So, since Grandpa Hawkeye was her mom's biological dad and this woman was her mom's biological mom, they must've been good friends when they were much younger. It seemed odd someone she only met today could have been friends with her grandpa years ago. It was even odder to think this woman she didn't know at all was really her grandma!

Suddenly, the woman lifted her hand and held it out to Jannah. Jannah bit her lip and sucked in a breath. She wasn't sure she wanted to touch the woman, but it was clear the woman wanted to touch her! Jannah slowly took the hand offered to her.

"Thank you," Donna whispered.

Jannah held the woman's hand. Maybe her grandma just wanted to make sure it was Jannah who had stayed. She would be able to tell by the size of the young girl's hand.

"So soft." A faint smile curved Donna's lips as her fingertips curled loosely around the child's hand.

Jannah smiled. She had been thinking the old woman's hand was kind of leathery. And the veins bulged. And there were wrinkles. And it had funny brown spots all over.

Caught in her reverie of the aged hands, Jannah looked up and found Donna's eyes opened and looking at her. The woman's eyes were a light blue but blurry, like she was looking through water. Wait! She *was* looking through water! There were tears slipping down her cheeks!

"Oh!" Jannah jerked back in her chair. "Should I get Grandpa?"

"No," Donna whispered. "Stay."

"Okay." Jannah relaxed her anxious grip on the woman's hand. "Do you want to talk?"

"Tucker," was the only word that Donna could utter.

"You want me to tell you more about Tucker?" Jannah guessed.

"Yes," Donna answered. Her eyes were closed again.

Jannah scooted the chair closer to the bed, so she could lean back in the chair and still hold Donna's hand. She pushed back into the chair with her toes and pursed her lips while she thought of more Tucker stories to tell.

"Well, Tucker is almost my best friend," Jannah began. "He sleeps right beside my bed, and he wakes me up in the morning when it is time for me to get ready for school. I don't know how he knows what time it is, but he is always right on time! Sometimes, he has to nudge me a couple times to make sure I'm really awake.

"When Grandpa walked with Mom to get me after school, he would let Tucker come with them. As soon as Tucker saw me coming out of the school, he ran to me and almost knocked me over. He was so glad to see me. I was glad to see him, too!" The memories of those days tugged at Jannah's heart. "That was a sad time for Mom, but it was a long time ago. I probably shouldn't tell you that part of the story."

"Do," prompted Donna.

"It is pretty sad."

"I know."

Jannah cocked her head sideways and looked straight at Donna. "You already know all about that, too?"

"Not everything," Donna countered.

"I might cry if I talk about it." Jannah looked away from the woman and swallowed the lump in her throat.

"That's okay."

"I haven't really talked about it with anyone," Jannah confessed.

"You need to."

Jannah took a deep breath. "Mom got hurt when Daddy killed himself. He didn't mean to do it, I know! But I was pretty mad at him for a while. But I missed him, too. And Mom was so sad all the time. And that made me sad. It was a long time before we could smile very much. But Grandpa Hawkeye was there. He took care of us. I love him so much!"

"Me, too." Donna sighed.

Jannah sat up straighter in her chair. "But you aren't married to Grandpa!"

"No," Donna agreed.

"And you still love him?" Jannah prodded.

"Yes."

"Why didn't you marry Grandpa?"

"Should have." Donna sighed. Jannah looked at her again. There were more tears sliding down her cheeks.

"Well, Grandpa told me when I was mad at my daddy we have to forgive people who hurt us. So, I think Grandpa has forgiven you. He must still like you a lot, or we wouldn't have come here to see you."

"A good man," Donna responded. Jannah nodded her head silently.

Jannah sat back in her chair, perplexed by the affection Donna had shared. Was Grandpa Hawkeye going to lose someone he loved now? Why did there have to be so much loss in life?

"Your mom?" Donna prompted.

"Mom?" Jannah remembered how angry she had been with her mother last night. It was hard to stay mad at her, though. Jannah could see her mother was sad to find this woman hospitalized. "Well, my mom is my very best friend. She was sad when my daddy and Jake died, but she is happier now." Jannah scooted to the edge of her chair and leaned close to the old woman. "And I think she is falling in love with Dr. Pat," she whispered.

"Do you mind?" Donna asked.

A heavy sigh escaped Jannah's lips. "I really like Dr. Pat, but I'm afraid something bad will happen to him if he marries my mom. Bad things always happen to the people I love." Jannah sniffled back her tears.

Donna struggled to turn her head toward Jannah. "Not always," she said. "She has you."

The door opened then, and the nurse came in to check the machines hooked up to Donna. "Everything going okay?" the nurse asked Jannah.

Jannah nodded. "We've just been talking."

"I think we need to let Donna rest a while," the nurse suggested. "Let me show you where your mom is."

Jannah slid out of her chair and placed Donna's hand on the bed. "I will be back later."

"Good," Donna whispered.

CHAPTER TWENTY-NINE

ELIZABETH CLICKED ON THE ANSWERING machine and listened to the recorded message for a third time. "This is Broadlawns Hospital in Riverton. We need to let you know your mother was brought to our hospital this morning by ambulance. Please give us a return call as soon as you get this message."

Elizabeth stood motionless at the window as the woman's voice rattled off the hospital number and the machine beeped at the end of the message. She knew she should pack a bag and head to the hospital. Would her mother even want to see her after receiving the letter? Did Elizabeth even want to see her mother? Very hurtful words were spoken. Her mother did not understand Elizabeth's confusion and sense of betrayal.

If this was a second stroke, would her mother even survive, let alone recuperate? If she made the trip to the hospital, should she take Kendra? It could be the last time Kendra would see her grandmother.

Elizabeth remembered Kendra's wish to take her keyboard to play her piano pieces for her grandmother. That had never happened. Elizabeth had never even tried to arrange it. She didn't want to risk the disapproval of her husband. There was no good reason she should let his opinions keep her from taking Kendra to see her grandmother; but Elizabeth had endured a very cold shoulder from him before, and she did not want to be the cause of it again.

Kendra would be home from school in a few minutes. Elizabeth knew she needed to make a decision. She had not even called the hospital to check on her mother's status. The guilt burned deep in her heart. It would be embarrassing at this point to try to excuse her delayed response to the phone message. She would just go and deal with the consequences of her letter when she got there.

She grabbed a bag from her closet and began selecting clothes to take. One night or two? Or a week? How long would she be gone? If she took Kendra and then needed to spend more time at the hospital, how would she get her daughter back for school? Her husband would not be pleased if he needed to make the trip to get Kendra. But he probably wouldn't be pleased, anyway, when Elizabeth told him she was going to be with her mother.

Questions swirled in her head. It shouldn't be this difficult of a decision! She should have been on the road to the hospital as soon as she heard the phone message the first time! Did her brothers know? It was not easy to get ahold of either one of them. Situations like this were left to her to handle.

A slight shadow in the doorway jerked Elizabeth away from her thoughts. She looked up and found Kendra watching her with a puzzled look on her face.

"Where are you going, Mom?"

"Grandma is in the hospital again," Elizabeth said as she returned to packing.

"Oh no!" Kendra replied. "Do you want me to go with you?" She hurried to her mother's side and wrapped her arms around her.

"I-I don't know," Elizabeth stuttered. She pulled open a drawer and picked out pajamas to pack.

"I want to go," Kendra decided. "Is that okay?"

Elizabeth turned and pulled the young girl close again. "The doctor told us after Grandma's first stroke that a second stroke would be likely, and it would be worse. I don't know if she will make it this time."

"I want to see Grandma again, Mom," Kendra pressed. "I will go get some clothes packed." She turned and was gone before Elizabeth could decide if taking her along was the right thing to do.

Elizabeth scribbled a note to leave on the kitchen counter for her husband. He needed to know where they had gone, but there was no doubt in her mind he would have chosen to send them alone, anyway. Even in an emergency such as this, she would make the trip to be with her mother without her husband at her side.

ELIZABETH PULLED INTO THE HOSPITAL parking lot just after dark. It had been a long drive. She glanced over her shoulder and found Kendra slumped into the corner with her favorite snuggle blanket tucked under her chin.

"We're here, honey," she whispered.

She gathered up her purse and keys, stealing a quick glance in the mirror. There hadn't been time to fix her make-up, and her hair was loose around her face. A deep breath escaped as she squared her shoulders, preparing herself for what was to come.

"Ready to go, Kendra?" she asked as the child stretched out a yawn.

"I'm ready." Kendra unfastened her seatbelt and repacked the few books she had brought along to pass the time. She was into chapter books now, and she devoured one after the other at an advanced speed for her grade.

"It looks like we go in right there." Elizabeth nodded toward the bright light over the door. They climbed out of the car, and Elizabeth clicked the locks.

They walked through the automatic entrance toward the information desk. The clerk looked up with a smile. "May I help you?"

"We are here to see Donna Wright," Elizabeth answered.

"Certainly! Are you family?"

"Yes, we are," Elizabeth said. "I am her daughter, and this is her granddaughter."

"Perfect!" the clerk responded. "There is a small waiting room not far from your mother's room. You can wait there if other family members are with her right now."

Elizabeth nodded her head. Other family members? Had this woman already directed Andrew or Jack to their mother's room? "Can you tell me how to find her room?"

"Of course!" The clerk pulled a copy of the hospital floor plan from a pile on the corner of her desk and walked Elizabeth through each step with a pen. She handed the marked path to Elizabeth with a warm smile.

"Thank you," Elizabeth said. "Let's head this way, Kendra."

The hallway between the two buildings seemed endless. There were many closed doors and not another person in sight. At last, the bright red sign for the elevators came into view, and Elizabeth pushed a button to go up to the fourth floor. The elevator door opened, and they stepped out into the quiet hush of the patient floor. Kendra tucked her hand into her mother's as they walked toward the nurses' station.

Three nurses sat behind the counter, their heads lowered to their computer's level as they documented the night's activities. When Elizabeth stepped close to the counter, they all looked up to offer her assistance.

"We are here to visit Donna Wright," Elizabeth stated.

"Are you family?" The closest nurse tipped her head, squinting her eyes as she studied the pair at the counter.

Elizabeth bristled at the repeated question. "Yes. I am her daughter, and this is her granddaughter."

The nurses looked at each other, then turned to face her again. One of the nurses stood. "I'm sorry, but Donna's daughter is already here. I'm confused."

Elizabeth took a step back and swallowed the lump in her throat. "Excuse me. What did you say?" She shook her head in disbelief.

"There is already a woman here who told us she is Donna's daughter. Does your mother have two daughters? Her contact information states she has two sons and one daughter."

Elizabeth closed her eyes, taking a deep breath before she answered. "My name is Elizabeth Ford. If you check my mother's information, I think you will find I am listed as her daughter."

A frown furrowed across the nurse's face. "I don't understand then. There is already a woman here who told us she is Donna's daughter. Does your mother have another daughter who is not listed in the patient information?"

The nurse reached for a patient chart and flipped back to the front sheet. Her eyes swept down the sheet to confirm the name of Donna's daughter. "Yes, here you are! Your name is listed here as a contact, as well as your two brothers, Jack and Andrew. There is also a James Hawthorne listed as a contact. But I don't see another daughter listed."

Elizabeth felt Kendra's eyes on her. She still held the small hand in her own. How could she explain to the nurse her mother did have another daughter when her own child did not even know that?

"Th-there must be some mistake," Elizabeth stammered. "I can show you my ID."

The flustered nurse turned to the other nurses behind the desk before agreeing. "If you have your ID available, that would help us."

Elizabeth unzipped her wallet and pulled out her driver's license. She handed it to the nurse, biting her tongue to hide her frustration.

"Thank you," the nurse said as she returned the card to Elizabeth. "I do apologize for the confusion. The doctor has ordered one visitor at a time; so let me show you to the waiting room, and I will see if your mother is alone."

Elizabeth followed the nurse down the hallway. Anger boiled inside her. Why would that other woman be here? How did the hospital contact her? How was Elizabeth going to explain to Kendra her grandmother had hidden another daughter and granddaughter from them for so many years?

The nurse halted at the door of the small waiting room. There was only an older gentleman and a young girl there. The nurse motioned for Elizabeth to wait in the hallway while she went in to talk to the man.

When the nurse returned, the man stepped out with her. He looked familiar to Elizabeth. She had seen him before at some point, but where? What was that man's name the nurse had said was on the contact sheet? James Hawthorne? And then, she remembered! He was the man who had come to her mother's door when Donna was still at the nursing home! That was him! James Hawthorne!

The nurse looked between the two of them, waiting for them to speak to each other. James offered his hand to Elizabeth, but she stood frozen in place.

"Hello, Elizabeth," James said. "I'm James Hawthorne. I met you a few months ago when I came to visit your mother."

Elizabeth fought back the anger rising in her throat. The puzzle was beginning to come together in her mind. This man must be the father of her mother's first child. Why were they here?

"Yes, I remember you now," Elizabeth said quietly.

The nurse cleared her throat to interrupt. "There is someone with your mother at this time. You are welcome to wait here. It shouldn't be much longer, and then you will be able to go in."

"Thank you, but we will wait here in the hallway." Elizabeth glanced at Kendra, whose eyes were on the other young girl seated in the small waiting room.

"No, please come in and wait with us," James encouraged. "There's plenty of room in here."

Elizabeth swallowed hard. She could not—*would* not—make a scene that would embarrass her daughter! She would have to explain all this to Kendra later. She harnessed her outrage and led her daughter into the waiting room.

Anxious to put the children at ease, James introduced Jannah. "This is my granddaughter Jannah. Jannah, this is Donna's daughter Elizabeth and, I assume, Donna's granddaughter?"

"Yes," Elizabeth stammered. "This is my daughter, Kendra." She placed a protective hand on Kendra's shoulder.

"Hi, Kendra!" Jannah greeted, oblivious to Elizabeth's cool demeanor.

"Jannah, why don't you scoot over here by me, and Elizabeth and Kendra can have that couch?" James pushed closer to the arm on his chair and made room for Jannah. Elizabeth and Kendra took their seats. Kendra raised her eyes enough to sneak a look at Jannah, and shy smiles bridged the gap between the two little girls.

CHAPTER THIRTY

MARTA REMOVED HER HAND FROM Donna's and stood to leave. Her mother had dozed off and was resting comfortably. She stood at the bedside and gazed at the face of the woman who had loved her enough to give her away. She could not imagine the agony of that decision!

Their conversation had been difficult. Donna's responses were short and uttered with great effort. She had thanked Marta for bringing Jannah and shed many tears. Marta found a tissue and wiped the tears from her mother's face. After that, Marta held her mother's hand, squeezing it gently to assure her she was still there.

The clock on the wall ticked away the fifteen minutes Marta had been allotted. She knew James would want some time, but the nurses would probably ask them to wait. Donna was sleeping, anyway. Maybe they could go find soda or coffee somewhere in the hospital.

"I love you, Donna," she whispered then turned to leave the room. She stepped into the hallway, shut the door, and leaned against the wall to catch her breath. It was becoming too familiar to her, this turning loose of someone dear to her. How would Jannah cope with this woman's death?

Marta checked in at the nurses' station. "She is sleeping now," she shared in a whisper and turned toward the waiting room.

Behind her, a nurse stood and called after her. "Excuse me, but didn't you say you are Donna's daughter?"

Marta halted and spun around to face the nurse. "Yes, I am. Is there a problem?"

"It's just that another woman checked in with us, and she said she is Donna's daughter. Her name is on the patient's release form."

"Oh! That would be Elizabeth," Marta responded. "Donna is my biological mother, but I was adopted at birth and only recently met her for the first time. I don't even know if Elizabeth knows about me. I'm so sorry for the confusion."

"It *was* confusing," the nurse agreed, "but it seems you are both daughters. Thank you for clarifying that for us."

"Thank you for letting me know Elizabeth is here," Marta answered. "Sounds like I need to get back to the waiting room and introduce myself."

James watched the clock and knew Marta would be returning soon. When her fifteen minutes were almost up, James stood. The tiny room had been much too quiet, and perhaps, if he stirred, the silence would break as well.

"I'm going to go find a cup of coffee," he said. "Elizabeth, would you like me to bring a cup for you?"

Elizabeth looked up from her hands. "No, thank you." She bent her head again, as if to dismiss his presence.

James smiled at her and then turned to Jannah. "Want to come with me, Jannah?"

"No, I'm fine," Jannah replied. "It's about time for Mom to come back, isn't it?"

James glanced at the clock on the opposite wall. "I think you're right! Maybe I will run into her in the hallway and see if she wants a coffee. How about you girls? Would you like a soda or juice?"

"Sure!" Jannah slid to the edge of her seat and wiggled her knees in and out. "Maybe an orange soda?"

"I'll see if they have that," James promised. "Kendra, anything for you?"

Kendra looked first at her mother, who simply nodded her head. "I'll have an orange soda, too, please. And thank you."

"Well, let's hope they have orange soda!" James laughed as he headed out the door.

As expected, James saw Marta leaving the nurses' station. He motioned for her to step aside at a telephone alcove.

"Where's Jannah?" Marta quizzed.

"She is waiting for you to get back. I'm just on a coffee and soda mission. I can grab one for you, too, if you want one. But I need to let you know we don't have the waiting room to ourselves anymore. Elizabeth and Kendra are here."

"Right. The nurses told me Elizabeth is here, but they didn't mention her daughter." Marta's eyebrows arched in contemplation. "I guess I hadn't thought about that happening. I wonder if Elizabeth knows about me?"

"I'm not sure," James answered. "I didn't explain our connections to Donna. I did run into her once at Donna's house, but even then, I didn't tell her how I knew her mother. She is very quiet. Maybe she knows."

"I guess I will just introduce myself and let it go until she asks questions about me," Marta decided. "Have the girls talked?"

James sighed. "No, not really. Jannah spoke to Kendra when they first came into the room, but that's it."

"Well, let me go see if I can get some communication going! I think I know a thing or two about getting kids to talk." She grinned as she headed toward the waiting room.

Marta peeked into the waiting room to get her bearings before entering. Having been introduced to Donna's granddaughter through a photograph, Marta knew Jannah and Kendra would be very close to the same age. There must be something they had in common. Once the kids were chatting, it would be much easier to get a conversation going between the adults.

Jannah spotted her before the others in the room. "Hey, Mom, you're back!" she announced. "Is Donna doing OK?"

Marta stopped in the doorway. "She is sleeping," she answered and then turned to the new visitors in the room. She stepped toward Elizabeth and held out her hand. "Hi! I'm Marta. It looks like you have already met Jannah."

Elizabeth ignored the handshake offered to her. "I'm Elizabeth. Donna is my mother," she said. It was matter-of-fact information and not accompanied by a welcoming smile.

"I'm glad to meet you, Elizabeth." Marta ignored the icy reception. "I'm sorry I was with your mother when you arrived. She is sleeping now, but I'm sure the nurses will allow you to go in to see her soon." She turned toward Kendra. "Let me guess—you are in fourth grade this year?"

Puffing up a bit at the miscalculation, Kendra corrected, "I'm in third grade."

"Oh!" Marta said. "That means you and Jannah are in the same grade!" The two girls looked at each other and giggled.

Marta grinned at the girls and then looked at Elizabeth. Her gaze had fallen again to her hands, and there was no acknowledgement of the interaction between the young girls. Was she sad about her mother? Or was she offended? It was obvious Elizabeth did not wish to carry on a conversation with her.

"Beep, beep," James quipped as he walked up behind Marta. "Coffee and sodas coming through!" Marta stepped out of the doorway to allow him to enter the waiting room.

"Lucky for you girls, the machine did have orange soda! Here you go!" The girls reached for their cans and popped them open.

"Thanks, Grandpa." Jannah licked the frosty orange from her upper lip after the first slurp.

"Yes, thank you," Kendra mimicked.

"You are both welcome!" James handed one coffee to Marta, then settled down on the couch next to Jannah, making sure there was room at the other end for Marta.

Marta caught his eye and cocked her eyebrow in Elizabeth's direction. The woman's eyes were still fixed on her hands in her lap. James shrugged his shoulders. Attempts had been made to welcome Elizabeth into the room, and she had chosen to withdraw. Marta knew James wanted to visit with Donna, but she was sure he would defer to Elizabeth when the nurse allowed another visitor.

Before long, the nurse stepped into the room. "I checked in on Donna, and she woke when I changed her IV bag. She would be glad to have another visitor."

Marta and James waited for Elizabeth to ask if she could go in to see her mother, but there was no reaction from her. "Elizabeth, I think your mother would be very glad to see you. How about if you take this turn?" James coaxed.

Elizabeth rearranged her jacket and purse over her arm and stood to leave. "Do you want to go in with me, Kendra?"

Before the child could answer, the nurse responded, "I'm sorry, but we are only allowing one visitor at a time."

"Kendra can stay here with us," Marta offered to Elizabeth. "Maybe she can go in after you?"

"Are you okay with waiting here, Kendra?" Elizabeth asked, turning her back to Marta.

Kendra looked around at the new faces around her. Jannah smiled at her and shook her head in encouragement. "I guess so," Kendra answered. Jannah jumped up and moved next to Kendra. Elizabeth clicked her tongue and disappeared down the hallway.

CHAPTER THIRTY-ONE

ELIZABETH SUCKED IN A DEEP breath when she saw her mother lying in the hospital bed. She dreaded approaching her. How did her mother feel about her now? They hadn't talked since she had received the letter. The letter had been angry, accusatory, and bridge-burning.

The nurse checked all the monitors, then motioned for Elizabeth to come closer. Donna's eyes were open, but she did not turn her head toward Elizabeth. Multiple tubes were attached to her mother. The beeping behind Elizabeth ticked off the seconds she was wasting just standing there.

"Hi, Mom," she whispered. "It's me—Elizabeth."

Donna lifted her hand. Elizabeth reached to accept her mother's plea for touch. Their hands melted together as if they had been formed exactly for this moment. Palm to palm, their fingers wrapped their hearts in an embrace otherwise not possible.

Whose tears fell first? Donna's or Elizabeth's? It hardly mattered, but then again, it did. Elizabeth longed to ask for forgiveness. She ached for her mother to sense the regret strangling Elizabeth's voice. In the far corner of her heart, though, she also clung to the betrayal she had felt at her mother's confession. The two emotions raged within her as she stood holding her mother's hand.

Elizabeth pulled a tissue from a box on the bedside table and dabbed at her eyes. Then she pulled a second tissue and gently wiped the tears streaking down her mother's cheeks. Her mother's fingers tightened around her own.

Donna's frail voice broke the silence. "I love you," she whispered.

"Oh, Mom!" Elizabeth replied through fresh tears. "I love you, too!"

"More than you know." Donna struggled to continue, a labored breath taken between each word. "I'm sorry," her mother wheezed.

This time, Elizabeth squeezed her mother's hand. Now, her tears fell unchecked. It was as if a dam had burst in Elizabeth's heart. She felt her legs crumple as she sank into the chair next to the bed. Her head bowed to her chest as the tears fled down her cheeks. Still, her hand clung to her mother's.

"I needed to tell you," her mother implored in a hoarse whisper.

"I know," Elizabeth replied.

"She is here," Donna continued.

"I know." Finally, the reality of the other daughter was acknowledged. But the assurance of her mother's love overcame the opposing reality of Elizabeth's anger. "It's okay," she added.

"She has her family." Donna continued laboring over each word. "I have you." Her fingers tightened slightly around Elizabeth's. "And Kendra?"

"She is here, too, Mom," Elizabeth assured her. "She will be in to see you next."

"Thank you." Donna's eyes closed then, and there was only silence.

Elizabeth jerked around to check the monitors. The heartbeats still zigzagged across the black screen. Elizabeth glanced at the wall clock. Her fifteen minutes had expired five minutes ago. Would she soon be ushered out of the room and expected to return to the waiting room filled with people she didn't know? She turned to her mother again and waited for a shallow breath to flutter her mother's chest. She tiptoed to the door and let herself out in search of a quiet place where she could gather her thoughts.

CHAPTER THIRTY-TWO

JAMES LISTENED AS THE CHILDREN got acquainted. He smiled at their animated comparisons of school teachers. Marta had not shared with Kendra that she herself was a teacher, so the discussion was unhampered by fears of insulting someone. He glanced at Marta and found her smiling at the girls, too.

"Do you have a dog?" Jannah asked, eager to tell her new friend about Tucker.

Kendra wrinkled up her nose. "Oh no! My daddy doesn't like pets. He says they make a house smell."

"Oh," Jannah's chipper voice fizzled into disappointment.

"Do you have a dog?" Kendra's curiosity prodded the conversation along.

Jannah could not help but perk up at the opportunity to talk about Tucker. "Yes! He is a yellow lab, and his name is Tucker. I wish you could meet him!" Jannah cocked her head as she considered how to describe her dog to Kendra. "He has three legs, but he is the best dog ever!"

"Just three legs?" Kendra's eyebrows arched in disbelief. "How does he walk with just three legs?"

Jannah nodded with enthusiasm. "Yep, just three legs. He was hit by a truck, and his hind leg was so damaged, Dr. Pat could not save it. But he fixed up Tucker, and now he can run and play as good as ever!"

"Does he have a dog house?" Kendra asked.

"No!" Shock at such an unthinkable arrangement spewed in Jannah's response. "Tucker stays in the house with Mom and me! He sleeps on the floor right beside my bed every night."

"Oh!" Kendra shook her head. "My daddy wouldn't like that at all."

Jannah pushed back in her seat. "I guess he probably wouldn't, but I can't imagine not having Tucker beside me every night. I would worry about him if he had to stay outside." She paused again, then turned to her mother. "I don't think Tucker makes our house smell, does he, Mom?"

Marta smiled at the girls. "Hmmm. Well, I don't notice a smell in our house. Sometimes, when we are really attached to a pet, we are able to overlook things other people might notice. If you don't have a pet, Kendra, what do you like to do when you aren't busy with school work?"

Now, it was Kendra's turn to smile. She sat on her hands at the edge of her seat and kicked her legs. "I play piano! And I take dance lessons. And French lessons, but I don't really like those." Her nose turned up in disgust.

"You know how to play the piano?" Jannah pressed with wide eyes.

Marta joined the conversation. "How old were you when you started piano lessons?"

"I was in kindergarten," Kendra replied, "but I started dance way before that!"

"Wow!" Jannah whispered. "You must have to practice something all the time!"

Kendra shrugged her shoulders. "I don't have anything else to do."

James heard the loneliness in the little girl's voice. Donna had told him Kendra was an only child. Really, Jannah was, too. It sounded like that might be the only thing the two girls had in common. Besides a common grandmother.

The nurse stepped into the doorway. "Donna is asking for Kendra," she said as she watched for a response from the two girls.

"Where's my mom?" Kendra whispered in a panic.

"I think she is making a phone call," the nurse replied. "We will probably run into her on our way to Donna's room." Kendra stood hesitantly, and the nurse motioned for the young girl to follow her.

Before they arrived at the nurses' station, Kendra saw her mother at the far end of the hallway. "Can I talk to my mom before I go in to see Grandma?" she asked the nurse.

"Sure!" The nurse stepped behind the station as Kendra hurried to her mother.

Kendra saw her mother dab at her eyes with a tissue as she approached. Her grandmother must be dying! Why else would her mother be so sad? "Mom, is Grandma okay?" she asked.

Elizabeth startled when Kendra stepped in front of her. She opened her arms, and Kendra stepped into her embrace. "It's just hard to see Grandma in a hospital bed again," she explained as she pulled her daughter close.

"Did she speak to you?"

"Yes. Speaking is difficult for her, but she knew it was me."

"Grandma is asking to see me. Can you please go in with me?" Kendra begged.

The fear in the child's voice tore at Elizabeth's heart. "Let's ask the nurse if they might allow it this one time," she whispered. She took the girl's hand, and they headed toward the nurses' station. With Kendra's hand still tucked into hers, she approached the first nurse who looked up from her work.

"My mother is asking to see her granddaughter. Could I please step into the room with her?" Elizabeth asked.

The nurse seemed to note the child's age and look of apprehension. "Our orders are for one visitor at a time for fifteen minutes. Your mother has suffered a severe stroke, and the order is in place to maximize her recovery options." She paused and turned to the other nurses at the station. "However, if you would remain just inside the room and allow your daughter to visit with your mother one-on-one, I think we could allow that this time."

Elizabeth smiled down at her daughter and squeezed her hand. "Thank you for considering the situation. May we go in now?"

"Sure," the nurse responded. "Let me go in with you and check the monitors." She jumped up and led them down the hallway.

Inside the patient room, the nurse assessed the IV bags and read the humming monitors. Finding Donna awake, the nurse announced another visitor. "Kendra is with me, Donna. You were asking to see her."

Donna sucked in a labored breath and raised her hand. The nurse motioned for Kendra to step closer. Elizabeth remained at the door, watching.

"Hi, Grandma," Kendra whispered. She placed her small fingers into the hand that reached for her.

"Kendra," her grandma sighed. "I've missed you."

"I've missed you, too, Grandma. I wish we didn't live so far from you."

"You're here now." Donna breathed heavily and squeezed the child's hand.

Kendra turned to her mother, an uneasy look on her face. She had never had the opportunity to grow close to her grandma. They didn't see her very often. Still, they were family, and Kendra understood they needed to be together.

"Thank you"—Donna's voice quivered with the effort of speaking—"for coming." Her chest heaved with each breath. "I love you."

Kendra bent low to catch her grandmother's words. "I love you, too."

"Keep playing," Donna whispered.

Kendra's brow furrowed as she turned to her mother again. What did her grandmother mean?

"The piano," Donna finished.

Kendra's face broke into a smile. "Oh, I will!" she assured her grandmother. "I wish you could have come to my last recital!"

"Me, too," Donna agreed. "Next time?"

"I hope so! I'm working on a very hard song."

"Keep practicing," Donna urged. Her eyes fluttered, and then her hand went limp in Kendra's.

Kendra glanced at the monitors beeping their nonsense behind her. She slipped her fingers away from her grandmother's hand and gripped the bedrail as she looked into the woman's face. She felt her mother watching and crying from the doorway and wondered if this was their goodbye.

CHAPTER THIRTY-THREE

JAMES AND MARTA SAT IN silence while Jannah watched a cartoon on the television in the waiting room. The absence of Donna's other daughter and granddaughter was almost refreshing. Elizabeth seemed unwelcoming, perhaps even suspicious of the others' right to be present. Like Marta, James had never considered they might all end up in the same waiting room. At some point, there would need to be an explanation for how they all fit into the puzzle. Would it become even more complicated if Donna's other children arrived?

James had not visited Donna alone yet. It was more important for the others to spend time with her first. Hospital rooms were familiar territory for him. As a pastor, he had spent many hours waiting, ministering, and praying. He had found, though, that all the experience was useless when the sorrow was personal. This sorrow was very personal.

His thoughts pulled him back to his high school days when he and Donna were teenagers incapable of seeing past the current moment's embrace. That moment of passion had resulted in a pregnancy that had caused so much turmoil. He had been denied contact with Donna, and she had been sent away from her home.

Months later, he had received the phone call from Donna that the baby had been born. Without a word to his parents, he had jumped into his car and driven half out of his mind to go see the baby.

He could still feel the gut-wrenching ache of peering through glass at his baby on the other side, knowing there was no chance for him to even touch the downy hair of the bundle wrapped in a pink blanket. The sound of Donna's sobs echoed in his memory, her heart crying because she could never hold her baby again. Years had passed as he wondered about the wellbeing of his daughter and kept the secret from his own wife, always fearing she would never understand.

As memory chased after memory, he remembered the day he had driven for miles to visit with Donna. From the pages of a Bible left behind, Donna had accepted Christ as her personal Savior. Then, James had been given the privilege of introducing Donna to both her firstborn child and the God Who loved her.

James leaned forward and held his head in his hands. There was no stopping the tears. His indiscretion all those years ago had led to this convergence of individuals with hidden relationships. Though if it had never happened, Marta and Jannah would not exist. God had allowed him joy in spite of the wrong he had done with Donna! Through his tears, he silently thanked his God for the forgiveness He had granted and for the unmerited blessings that had followed.

James felt a warm arm around his shoulder. Marta pulled a tissue from the box on the stand beside her chair and handed it to him. James wiped at his tears and shook his head at the realization the baby who had been deemed a "mistake" by others was now the woman who offered him comfort.

The clock in the waiting room ticked away the minutes. Marta watched as Elizabeth and Kendra returned and took their seats across from her. It was clear that Elizabeth had been crying. Her daughter held onto her hand and darted looks at her mother's face, eager to console.

James sat back in his seat, stretched his arms above his head, and smiled at Marta. He patted his knees and then stood. "How about you two girls go for a walk with me? I need to stretch my legs!"

Jannah jumped up and hurried to his side. "Want to come, Kendra?"

Kendra hesitated and looked to her mother for approval. Finally, Elizabeth spoke. "Go ahead if you want."

"I say we look for a vending machine that sells something besides coffee! What do you girls think?" James and the girls headed out the door.

Marta and Elizabeth sat in an awkward silence. Perhaps it was time to explain her presence. Perhaps that was why James had left them alone.

"Elizabeth, I need to tell you why I am here," she began.

"I know who you are!" Elizabeth snapped. "My mother has told me about you."

The resentment in Elizabeth's words felt like a slap to Marta's face. Marta swallowed the lump in her throat. "I see," she said. "I met your mother for the first time only a couple days ago. My daughter met her just today."

"I don't understand why any of you felt like you needed to be here now." Elizabeth shook her head and clicked her tongue.

"James is my father, and I came partly to support him," Marta explained. "But I also brought Jannah because Donna had told me she would like to meet Jannah."

"Donna? Why do you call her 'Donna'? She is your *mother*!" Elizabeth stared at Marta, her eyes sparking with anger.

"Well, while Donna is my biological mother, I consider the woman who adopted me to be my 'mother,'" Marta contended. "Donna seems to understand."

"My impression was that she was thrilled to find her long-lost daughter," Elizabeth answered.

Marta paused before answering. "Is that so difficult to understand? Really?" she asked softly. "Would you not want to know what had happened to your child if you had not seen the child for many years?"

"There is no way I would ever have abandoned a child, so I would never have found myself in that situation!"

"But what if you had no choice? What if someone else made the decision for you?"

"Oh, my mother had a choice! She could have kept you!"

A heavy sigh escaped from Marta's heart. "I, for one, am glad Donna made the decision she made. At that point in her life, she was not able to provide for me. I was adopted by a very loving couple, and I have had a wonderful life. Your mother was pleased to hear me say that." Marta hesitated before adding, "That was all Donna wanted from me—to know I was happy and that I did not hate her for placing me for adoption."

Elizabeth's brow furrowed as she asked, "You don't hate her?"

"No, I definitely don't hate her," Marta assured her. "Nor do I expect her to make any restitution to me for giving me up. There is no need. I have parents who love me, and my daughter has grandparents who dote upon her."

"Then *why* are you here?"

"Because Donna wished to meet my daughter, and I was afraid this might be the last opportunity." Marta felt like she was using her teacher voice to repeat the explanation. "And because James, my biological father, cares very much for Donna, and I didn't want him to be alone. The hospital called him when your brothers were too far away to get here soon and they could not reach you."

"You and James seem very close. How long have you known he is your father?" Elizabeth asked.

Marta smiled. "Yes, James has become an important part of my family. He has been our neighbor for about three years, but he didn't tell me he was my father right away. In fact, it was about a year after he moved in that he told me. It caused a lot of friction for us, but he was there to help us through some pretty rough times a few years ago. He had his reasons for not disclosing his identity right away, and I have forgiven him. The relationship we had developed was too important to discard it without listening to his reasons. He and Jannah are almost inseparable now."

Elizabeth leaned back in her chair and crossed her arms. "I don't understand why my mother didn't tell me about you years ago," Elizabeth confessed.

"Maybe, like James, she has reasons she has not shared with you yet. Sometimes, a secret gets buried under so much regret, the very idea of digging it out and sharing it becomes more of a burden than a person can bear," Marta suggested. "I would guess your mother tried to tell you many times, but she was afraid to hurt you or jeopardize her relationship with you."

"It might have hurt less if she had told me before we got to this point." The anger seemed to be gone from Elizabeth's words, replaced with overwhelming perplexity.

"Maybe," Marta agreed. She tipped her head, her lips knit in thought before continuing. "I am sorry it hurt you to find out about me. I do not intend to make any claims on your mother's family. My adoptive family gave me a loving home, and I chose to meet your mother specifically to assure her of that."

"She does seem very relieved to know," Elizabeth admitted. "I wrote a very cruel letter to my mother after she told me about you. I almost decided not to come here after I listened to the message on my phone. I have been so angry with my mom. I wasn't sure she would even want to see me, but we apologized to each other a few minutes ago. It would have been awful if she had passed away with that still between us."

"I'm glad you decided to come. And it must be a relief to have settled things with your mother." Marta smiled. "I haven't known Donna long, but she seems like someone who would be compassionate enough to consider the perspective of others. And I can tell you, for certain, she loves you very much. She has tried for many years to protect you from the secret she felt she had to hide. We are both mothers now. We know how fiercely we protect our children. It's what moms do."

Elizabeth nodded her head. Her lips turned up slightly as she met Marta's gaze, the sisters' eyes both brimmed with tears.

CHAPTER THIRTY-FOUR

JANNAH AND KENDRA RETURNED TO the waiting room with a bag of chips and a candy bar apiece. They found a seat together and nibbled on their snacks between giggles as they whispered about how James' fist had persuaded the vending machine to cough up their selections.

"The nurse said I could go in to visit Donna now," James told Marta when he returned with the girls. He headed down the hallway to Donna's room. He pushed the door open and stood inside the room, waiting for his heart to calm before approaching the bed. The humming monitors beckoned him closer.

"It's me, Donna," James said softly.

Donna's eyes struggled to open. "Finally," she responded. A faint smile curved her lips.

"Several people wanted to see you," James countered. "I had to wait my turn."

"Thank you"—Donna's breathing heaved between words—"for bringing Jannah." She lifted her hand, and James wrapped his fingers around her slim palm.

"It was Marta's idea to bring her," James admitted. "It was time for me to share her with you. She's not just mine. She is mine to share."

"Thank you," Donna repeated.

James pulled the bedside chair closer and sat down. "Elizabeth and Kendra have been in the waiting room with us," James began. "Is everything okay between you and Elizabeth?"

"It is now." Donna sighed. "I should have told her sooner." She breathed deeply and then continued. "How is Tucker?"

"Good as new!" James reported.

"Good." Donna sighed again. "Doctor . . . said he would recover." It happened then. Donna looked at him and held his eyes long enough for him to know it had been she who paid the large vet bill. James' eyes widened as he pieced the story together. "But how did you know which veterinary clinic took care of Tucker?"

Donna looked at him again, this time her eyes admitting she had been found out. "I called," she admitted, "many places."

James put his free hand over hers and patted it tenderly. "That was so kind of you," he whispered. A tear slipped down her cheek before she looked away. A thought crept into James' head. Maybe there was more that Donna had done. "And the house loan?" His eyes narrowed as he waited for her response.

"The l-least I could do," Donna stammered.

James thought back to the horrible stress Marta had been under before her house mortgage was mysteriously paid off. Marta had never shared with him the balance of the mortgage loan, but it had to be considerable. "You have no idea how relieved Marta was when the bank told her she owed nothing! And perplexed! She could never figure out who did such an incredible thing for her!"

"The least I could do," Donna repeated.

James tightened his grip on Donna's hand. "I was relieved as well. Your secret gift meant Marta and Jannah did not have to move. Thank you for that!"

"She needs you." Donna closed her eyes and swallowed.

"I need her." James nodded. "And Jannah, too! I would have missed them so much if they had moved. Thank you for doing that for her."

Another weak smile curved Donna's lips. "You're welcome."

"Did you tell Marta?" James asked.

"No."

"May I?" James pressed.

"Sometime. Later." Donna closed her eyes tightly in sudden pain, her breathing labored more than before. The beeping of the monitors became irregular. "Have a Bible?" she asked.

"Of course!" He reached inside his jacket to retrieve the small Bible.

"Read to me."

James turned to a favorite spot in his Bible and began reading, "'Do not let your hearts be troubled. You believe in God; believe also in me. My Father's house has many rooms; if that were not so, would I have told you that I am going there to prepare a place for you? And if I go and prepare a place for you, I will come back and take you to be with me that you also may be where I am.'"

"Thank you," Donna whispered. An aura of peace shone through her wrinkled face.

"That was from John 14. I have another verse I want to share with you." James closed his Bible and began to quote the verse that had guided his heart for so much of his life. "'And we know that in all things God works for the good of those who love him, who have been called according to his purpose.'"

"Romans 8:28," Donna murmured. She jerked her hand away from James and grabbed at her chest. Her mouth opened, and she gasped in pain. Before James could reach for the call button, her hand fell back to her side, and her eyes closed, the anguished furrows smoothed from her brow. The beeping monitors slowed to a monotone. She was gone.

James' head dropped to the bed, where he still held Donna's hand. He swallowed the tears at the back of his throat. This moment was inevitable, but sorrow trumped the logical expectation that Donna would not survive this stroke. His heart retreated to his source of peace. Donna was a child of God, and she was home now—safely home.

CHAPTER THIRTY-FIVE

JAMES PULLED UP BESIDE THE Jeep parked on the side of Marta's driveway. Jannah threw open her door and raced to the front step to accept Tucker's slobbery welcome. It was a happy reunion, but Pat's eyes were drawn to the woman walking up the driveway toward him. Marta had called to tell him about her mother's passing, and he knew her emotions would be raw.

Marta's smile was wide, but her cheeks were moist. Pat spread his arms, and she melted against his chest as he pulled her close. He buried his nose in her hair and breathed in the scent of her perfume. He felt her heart pounding against his, pouring out the sorrow she had dammed up inside until this moment.

Pat turned his head to check on Jannah. She sat on her knees with her arm around Tucker's neck and was watching her mother. There was no anger on her face. Instead, there was a shy grin that seemed to acknowledge her mother's need for the kind of love Jannah had found with Tucker. Pat winked at her, and she nodded her head.

"Let's go, Tucker!" Jannah jumped up and ran toward the backyard, the lopsided dog in close pursuit.

James carried the overnight bags to the step and set them down. He placed a hand of approval on Pat's back and then walked quietly back to his car. Pat squinted his eyes shut and silently thanked God. He knew somehow, God would ease the memories of the fallen child he had cradled in his arms. God would give Marta the courage to love again. God would make room in Jannah's heart for another man to be her father. And James would always be there as his friend. Gratitude swelled in his heart. Those three special people had helped heal him. And it was all because of a three-legged dog.

EPILOGUE

JAMES STEPPED BACK FROM THE casket and waited for the mourners who had come to the cemetery to pay their final respects to the family. It was a warm autumn day, and the sun had done what it could to make the day bearable. Colored leaves glided on the breeze to their final resting places among the gravestones.

James noticed a lone figure move toward the seated family, closing the short gap that had been maintained from the others who were speaking soft words of condolence. James recognized the man from a picture on Donna's mantel, the man who had been simply introduced as "the children's father." Donna's oldest son stood as the man approached. Father and son embraced, the moment sealed with a tender pat on the shoulder of the navy uniform. The man moved toward Elizabeth and knelt to take her hand. He covered her slim fingers with his free hand and lifted his eyes to the damp face of his daughter. He tilted his head and offered a soft smile in recognition of her sorrow. Standing again, the man reached for the outstretched hand of his third child. Their hands locked in grips of earned respect, and they nodded to each other as the man stepped away.

James turned from the family, denying any right to participate in their common grief. He watched small groups of mourners return to their cars, their voices still muffled in respect. His responsibilities in the service were nearly complete. His years as a minister had required funeral services for many different parishioners. Some services had been particularly difficult, but today's was unique. There was deep satisfaction in having joined a dear friend with both her estranged daughter and her eternal Savior. If only the mother and daughter had been given more time together.

A stray giggle caught James' ear, and he turned to find Jannah and Kendra standing together near a gravestone across the walkway. Their hands were joined, and their heads bobbed closer as they shared the thought that prompted the laughter. James allowed a faint smile of his own. There were no disapproving glances from either of the girls' mothers, and for that, James was grateful. Every funeral needed children for the reminder that life would go on, complete with giggles.

Marta and Pat had held back from the line; but the crowd had thinned, and now, James watched them approach the family. Pat held her close with his arm around her waist. When they came face to face with Elizabeth, Marta leaned down and wrapped her arms around her grieving sister. The embrace was prolonged. Whispers between them bridged the gap years of secrecy had forged. There was much for them to learn about each other, but there was time for that. Peace had been made.

DEBBIE GILLILAND HAS BEEN A closet writer most of her adult life. Publishing a book was always at the top of her bucket list, and that dream was fulfilled with the release of her first book, *To Comfort a King*. Since that time, *Mine to Love*, the first book in this series, was published. A third book in the series is being planned. Debbie and her husband enjoy touring their home state of Iowa on their Gold Wing motorcycle and supporting their grandchildren in their many academic and athletic events.

CONTACT INFORMATION
www.debbiejgilliland.com
debbiejgilliland@yahoo.com
www.facebook.com/debbiejgilliland

MINE to Love

a novel

DEBBIE GILLILAND

James Hawthorne, a widowed and recently retired minister, has searched for and found his only child, given up for adoption at birth. Leaving behind his congregation, he purchases a house next to his daughter, Marta, now an adult with a family of her own.

James longs to reconnect with Marta, but secrets and tragedy force him to question everything. Tracking down the biological mother, he finds a broken woman who is weary of living. Of all the souls he has ministered to, the mother of his child is the last person he ever expected to help. In his quest for answers, she reveals information that both devastates James and sets him free.

Beset by uncertainty and doubt, James must rely on faith, love, and his belief in family. Already very attached to Marta and her child, he knows they need him more than ever. But will he ever know for certain if he is Marta's father? Will he ever have the family he has secretly wept for all of his adult life?

Ambassador International's mission is to magnify the Lord Jesus Christ and promote His Gospel through the written word.

We believe through the publication of Christian literature, Jesus Christ and His Word will be exalted, believers will be strengthened in their walk with Him, and the lost will be directed to Jesus Christ as the only way of salvation.

For more information about
AMBASSADOR INTERNATIONAL
please visit:

www.ambassador-international.com
@AmbassadorIntl
www.facebook.com/AmbassadorIntl

Thank you for reading this book!

You make it possible for us to fulfill our mission,
and we are grateful for your partnership.

To help further our mission, please consider leaving us a review on your social media,
favorite retailer's website, Goodreads or Bookbub, or our website.

Betty is sure that Ida Lou does not belong in their church when the woman shows up to the Good Friday service with her small dog in tow. But before she knows what's happening, Betty—along with the other women of the WUFHs (Women United For Him)—is pushed into helping the woman. God works in mysterious ways—and through ordinary people. The town of Prosper is about to experience some drama—and it all starts with a dog who comes to church.

Niamh is a devout Catholic living with her parents in Ireland in 1908. She has never doubted their faith, but when she joins a suffragist movement, Niamh suddenly finds herself being introduced to women from who all believe that women deserve to be treated as well as men. As Niamh begins to imagine a world where women and men are equal, she meets Fred, the brother of one of her sister suffragists. Based on a true story, The Last Letter is a tale of overcoming prejudice and finding love against all odds.

Sam Anthem has always been a team player, leading his Home Team on secret missions around the world. When he is forced on a vacation, he is introduced to a former covert ops soldier-turned pastor. But the vacation takes a turn when the Home Team comes under attack. As the team fights to stay alive against an unknown adversary, Sam begins to wonder if there is more to life than just the job. With his life on the line, Sam must decide between the job or his newfound faith and possible love.